Four Square Miles
the dream

Four Square Miles

A story of pride, love, family, and a dream.

KEITH MICHAEL PRESTON

ISBN: 978-1-7345925-2-8

Cover Art Designed by Thomas J. Zaffo/B. DeAngelo

Typesetting & Layout by Monte Press Inc.

Printed in the U.S.A.

I am forever grateful to my spouse, Nancy Preston, my mother, Diane Preston, and father, George Preston for their continued support.

I would like to show appreciation to the following individuals for their invaluable advice and ongoing support while creating this book: Caroline Adams, Annette Nasti-Coppola, Marie Miserendino, and Amy Corcoran.

FOUR SQUARE MILES is a series that takes place in a suburb of New York City.

the dream is the third book of the series.

CHAPTER 1

It's early Sunday morning and Nutsy and Blackie are nervously waiting outside the hospital room of Blackie's husband, Ladro. He was rushed to the local hospital by an ambulance after Blackie had found him unconscious on their kitchen floor when she returned home from the grocery store last night.

The night before, a large amount of cash was stolen from Squalo's wall safe and all fingers pointed to Ladro, since he's a known and successful thief from back in the day.

Squalo convinced Vito to break into Ladro's house and search for his missing cash, so Vito drove over to Ladro's place and waited outside in his parked car to make sure the coast was clear. When he saw Ladro leave and was certain the house was unoccupied, Vito broke in through a side door.

Ladro realized he had forgotten something while on his way to meet Nutsy and when he went back into his house, Vito was already inside snooping through the kitchen cabinets.

Ladro heard an odd creaking sound behind him when he walked back into his kitchen and quickly turned drawing his pistol. Startled, Vito frantically snatched an empty beer mug off the counter and smashed it across Ladro's head.

Ladro had pulled the trigger but the magazine was empty, which was ironic because that was the reason he returned back home. After getting smashed over the head with the beer mug, Ladro stumbled backwards, smacked his head on the edge of the glass kitchenette table and crashed face down on the ceramic floor.

At the hospital, a doctor and a few nurses are now tending to Ladro who recently flatlined. Nutsy and Blackie are both silent and in shock while nervously waiting in the hospital hallway to see if Ladro pulls through or not. At this point, neither Nutsy nor Blackie know for sure who's responsible, but both suspect who's behind it.

Nutsy remains silent since he's nervous about his right-hand man pulling through. He's well aware that Blackie knows he had given Ladro the nod to perform the heist and it's not sitting right with her.

Ladro hit Squalo's safe, the main bookie of The Plains, and is secretly stashing a large amount of cash in the walls of his house. This cash is money being accumulated by Nutsy's old group of bookies for an apparent new hotel being built on the grounds of a racetrack in The Hills area. They were attempting to gather up one million dollars between the four of them to buy in and become investors.

The prior group was comprised of Nutsy, Squalo, Belo, and Donnola. The other three bookies have become envious as each watches their own profits steadily decline in their controlling areas, while Nutsy's sports gambling business has been thriving because of the populated and close-knit city he operates in.

They gave Nutsy an ultimatum to share in his success or else they would no longer accept any of his layoff bets. They know that if Nutsy is heavy on a game the wrong way he could become vulnerable without their support. Nutsy in so many words, told them to screw off which has upset his wife and father-in-law, since they both want Nutsy to take the safe way and give up some of his profits.

Kathy already experienced a time when Nutsy had operated by himself and got hit for a large amount of money from a football game. After slowly and painfully recovering, Nutsy formed this group to help layoff bets between each other. It had been working fantastically until the group decided to shake Nutsy down. It has recently come to everyone's attention that besides this proposal, Squalo seems to have his own agenda.

Years back, Squalo was the main bookie in The Vern and his son, Leo, controlled a local illegal group and a business. Leo was running narcotics and arms out of the business which made the big players of the city concerned, so they had Leo pinched and Squalo run out of town.

The city switched hands because of a few political moves Nutsy's father-in-law, Billy, had made. Since Squalo and Leo were making a mess of the city, Billy convinced the developers who were investing a tremendous amount of money at that time to help push them out. Billy also knew this would be a great avenue to help shift Nutsy to the top, which it did.

The police eventually pinched Leo and made Squalo's life unbearable. Squalo then decided to give The Plains a shot and manipulated his way to the top. The only difference is The Plains is a city that has developed tremendously into a commercial powerhouse. Many residents call it a mini Manhattan and don't have a need for a local bookie.

All these years, Squalo bit his tongue patiently waiting for his time. He feels his time has finally arrived since Leo just made parole and could provide some muscle behind his agenda.

Leo was able to slip through the cracks of the criminal justice system and was recently released from jail early because of state laws that had just been passed. Leo is one person who should not be on the streets and proved it last night, on his first night out. He dumped Vito, a young up-and-coming wannabe, into the woods just because he thought that Vito had screwed up and should've finished Ladro off.

Although Squalo loves the aggressiveness of his son, he was hoping to handle this in a different manner. Squalo has become a master manipulator and only cares about taking over Nutsy's sports betting operation with Leo's reputation behind him. Leo though, has his own agenda and is seeking redemption.

As the doctor and nurses attempt to revive Ladro, Nutsy paces in the hallway while Blackie leans up against a wall staring at an EXIT sign. She appears to be deep in thought, but it's quite the opposite. Her mind is overwhelmed with many thoughts and she is very frazzled.

A few minutes later, the doctor walks into the hallway and pauses by Nutsy and Blackie. They immediately think the worst but the doctor hesitantly says, "We got him back, but he's weak. No visitors in the room until we say so."

While Nutsy lets out a sigh of relief, Blackie tilts her head up toward the ceiling and whispers to herself, "Thank you."

"Let him rest," the doctor says while walking away.

Nutsy hugs Blackie and says, "He's gonna be alright. I know it. He ain't going down like this."

"I need some fresh air," Blackie says while heading toward the elevator.

Nutsy leans against the wall right outside of Ladro's room and wipes the sweat from his forehead. "Blackie, Nutsy, you out there?" Ladro softly says from his bed.

As Nutsy peeks into the room, Ladro softly asks, "What the hell are you doing, playing hide and seek?"

"Jesus Christ. Ya had us shittin' a brick out here." Nutsy peeks back to see if anyone at the nurses' station is looking and enters the room.

Ladro asks, "Where's Blackie?"

"She went downstairs to get some air. She's really upset. Ya fuckin' flatlined before."

"No wonder why."

"No wonder why, what?"

"You're never gonna believe what flashed through my mind for a minute."

"Just get some rest. I'm not even supposed to be in here."

"Fuck that... take a guess where we were?"

"Manhattan, gettin' a dirty water hot dog... how the hell am I supposed to know?"

Ladro laughs and replies, "I can go for one of those. No, you and me, we were running the biggest baseball complex on the east coast... it was beautiful."

"Just relax, will ya. You're talkin' nonsense now."

"Hear me out before I lose the thought. There was also a section for kids with special needs to play. N-J was throwing gas on the mound."

As Nutsy's eyes open wide, Ladro notices a gleam and continues, "Jesus Christ... that's it! How the hell didn't I see this?"

"See what?" Nutsy asks.

"I know you're secretive about it, but –"

A nurse enters the room and says, "Excuse me, sir, but the doctor doesn't want any visitors for the time being."

Ladro replies, "Give me five minutes with him, it's important."

Nutsy replies, "Just relax. I'll come back later."

"No!" Ladro turns to the nurse and says, "Five minutes."

She hesitantly replies, "Two," and walks out.

"Your dream, Nutsy, that's what it is."

"I don't know what you're talkin' about." Ladro hit it on the head, but Nutsy doesn't want to commit to it.

So Ladro asks, "Alright, you're playing dumb with me now. You do this bullshit all the time. What are the three things I know you love?"

"Chocolate chip cookies, crumb buns, and red wine."

Ladro laughs and replies, "Alright, go ahead, play games… no… baseball, that fucking dump for whatever reason, and donating to charities."

"Where are ya going with this?"

"That's what you want, Nutsy. You want this park to be about kids with special needs…"

Nutsy's eyes light up again and he can't believe Ladro had seen this vision since it's similar to what Nutsy has been envisioning. "Holy shit! You gotta see the spark in your eyes. It's like a lightning bolt just struck the room," Ladro says.

"Listen, I'm just glad ya woke up."

"Bullshit! I don't know what just happened to me, but we did it, Nutsy. It was like paradise. Shit, we even had on shorts and T-shirts like the old days when we walked around the baseball fields. Take a guess what shirt you had on?"

Nutsy just shrugs and Ladro continues on, "That Zeppelin one you used to wear all the time."

"I loved that one."

"Yeah, I know. I had the Floyd one on."

"Shit… talk about a fuckin' concert, ha?"

"Yeah, you ain't shitting. You're gonna love this. Across a wall was a big sign that said Gento's Sports Complex."

Nutsy's totally caught off guard and doesn't know how to respond. The nurse walks in and says, "Sir, please."

"One more minute," Ladro insists.

While the nurse shakes her head and leaves the room, Ladro continues on, "You don't have to admit it, I already know it. You always said the eyes tell the soul and yours just lit up like the tree at Rockefeller Plaza."

Nutsy is dumbfounded and Ladro knows it, so he presses on. "Look at you, you're fucking speechless… I thought hitting the safe would put me on the map forever, but doing this, we'll be legends, like fucking pioneers."

"I think the fall made ya a little nutty." Nutsy still doesn't want to commit since he's a superstitious man and doesn't have the details figured out as of yet.

"You and me, we'll make it happen. I already got the down payment stashed in my walls."

"Forget about this. What happened last night?"

Ladro blows off the question and replies, "Listen, we both have guilt in life, but we can leave this earth knowing we did something right… something legal for once in our lives for Christ Sake."

"Where are we going? This is all we know."

"I know one thing. Being successful doesn't mean you're significant in life."

"There's no difference. We all wind up in the same box."

"True… but your name either continues on, or it gets buried in that box. That's the difference of living a life of significance or chasing your tail to the end. We follow that dream of yours, and our names will never die."

"Enough of the philosophy, I asked ya what happened?"

"That young punk was snooping around my house."

"Who, that kid Vito?"

"Yeah, don't tell Blackie. I'm gonna settle this on my own when I get the fuck outta here."

"Ya couldn't get your piece out in time?"

Ladro remains quiet since he screwed up and forgot to snap in a new magazine and feels somewhat embarrassed.

"Oh yeah, ya made a rookie mistake. I told ya to lay off that shit," Nutsy says.

Blackie charges in and excitedly wraps her arms around Ladro's neck. "Ahhhh!" Ladro yells out.

Blackie leans back and asks, "What's wrong?"

"My fucking head's killing me. That's what's wrong."

Nutsy laughs and replies, "He sounds alright to me. I'll give ya time alone." Nutsy moves toward the doorway.

"Nutsy!"

Nutsy turns and nods.

"You'd love it. Bright green sod outfield, seats for the families, concession stand, and a beautiful electronic scoreboard. It was a perfect vision."

Blackie asks, "What are you talking about?"

"I think the fall fucked his mind up a little," Nutsy says.

Ladro laughs it off. "Yeah, it sure did. I see it clear as day now… take a guess who was running the scoreboard?"

"You," Nutsy sarcastically replies.

"Wrong. It was Sammy and N-J's girlfriend."

"N-J doesn't have a girlfriend. Get some rest." Nutsy walks out.

Blackie asks, "What are you mumbling about?"

"It's a secret between us."

"No more secrets or I'll kick both of your asses. I'm fed up with you two."

While Ladro laughs it off, Blackie continues on, "I'm not screwing around, Ladro. This is bullshit right now. You shouldn't even be in here."

The nurse walks in and pauses with her hands on her hips with an annoyed look. "Didn't I say only two minutes?"

"Give me thirty more seconds and close the door behind you. I gotta take care of my wife before she leaves."

Blackie glances toward the nurse who is attempting to hold back a smile and says, "I can tell he's better. He's acting like an asshole now."

CHAPTER 2

Squalo sits at his white kitchen table deep in thought. The fact that his son had just gotten out on parole and already tossed aside an up-and-coming wannabe, is not sitting right with him. The worst is, he witnessed the whole thing. Squalo has been eager to take back control of Nutsy's sports betting business and knew his son could help him achieve it, but not this way, not yet.

Leo wanders into the kitchen and says, "Wow! That was the best night's sleep I've had in years."

"That's great… I've been up all night thinking about the punk you just chucked in the woods."

"Fuck that kid… he wasn't gonna last anyway with his shitty attitude."

Squalo remains quiet and turns away.

"What time's that fundraiser?" Leo asks as he pulls a coffee mug out of a white cabinet.

"I don't know if I'm going."

"We gotta go. It's a dead giveaway if we don't."

"It starts around one. I'm more concerned about the late game anyway."

Leo laughs and replies, "You should be in Naples or some other place like that. Why are you bothering with all this bullshit?"

"Why are you?"

"Because I was screwed, that's why."

"Oh, it's alright YOU were screwed, but I guess not for me."

Leo peeks around and replies, "Yeah, I'd love to be screwed like this, sitting in a luxury high-rise with designer cabinets and wood floors throughout."

"What I have, I've worked hard for. The issue is what's been taken from me."

"Then we both have our own concerns, but some are gonna have to pay in a different way for me."

"Yeah, I can already tell that. I'll give you two months tops and you'll be back in eating dog shit again… don't go anywhere I gotta go to the bathroom."

"I don't have a car, remember?"

"Yeah, thanks for reminding me." Squalo snatches his key ring off of the kitchen counter and heads toward the bathroom.

Papo moves through his Venetian style bedroom slipping on his shirt when his cell phone buzzes on his bed. He notices Paulie's name on the display and answers, "This can't be good. My younger brother never calls this early."

Paulie currently lies on a lounge chair gazing at the Atlantic Ocean from his backyard patio on the Island and replies, "You know this guy's back on the street, right?"

"Yeah, I know." Papo slips on his designer watch.

"You discuss this with Nutsy yet?"

"Yeah."

"And?"

"He hasn't committed to anything."

"I can't wait too long with this, Papo. I got my own people to answer to."

"I know."

"If I gotta get my family involved, I will."

"I told you already. This has to be handled from the inside of these walls. That's how this city runs."

"My family has three mill on the line right now. If this derelict screws it up, I'll wind up like Bugsy in some field somewhere. And that ain't gonna happen."

"Just be patient, things don't happen overnight like the old days." Papo hangs up.

Squalo roams into the living room after hitting the bathroom and says to Leo, "I gotta say, I thought you would've learned by now."

Leo replies while sitting on the couch, "Learned what?"

"You come right out and toss this kid away? That's what a fucking moron would do."

Leo just laughs.

"Yeah, keep laughing… they should've never released you. I guess this is what happens when a degenerate slips through the cracks."

Leo sparks up. "Who the fuck are you kidding?! I'm the one who adds the tension around here, not that fucking weasel, Donnola, or that pretty boy, Belo."

"That's not the point. The person who learns is the one who lasts in the end."

"Oh yeah, what the fuck have you learned? You couldn't wait for me to get out and help you with this bullshit."

"You see, that's where you and I think differently. This fucking kid was good to take the rap for something and now you wasted it."

"You're right. We do think differently because I'm not taking the chance on Nutsy finding out we sent that punk to Ladro's house."

Squalo stands up and replies, "You better stay clean from now on. Shoot off your mouth all you want, but no more unnecessary bullshit like last night. You hear me?"

"I'll tell you what, I'll make a deal with you. The day I can buy myself an apartment like this, I'll calm down, how about that?"

Squalo shakes his head and replies, "Revenge is a dangerous thing. It fucks the revenger more than the revenged."

"You sound like the pot calling the kettle black."

"I'm not looking for revenge, it's a business move."

Leo laughs and replies, "Okay, keep on telling yourself that."

Billy sits in the exquisite backyard of Gloria's house in an upscale Westchester County community. She has approximately an acre of immaculately pruned and lush landscaping. A large pool and stone waterfall are surrounded by a limestone patio.

While Billy takes a sip of coffee and gazes at the waterfall, Gloria places a blueberry pie on the patio table and asks, "It's mesmerizing, isn't it?"

"I could stare at it all day."

"Trust me, after a while it becomes like everything else."

Billy glances around and says, "I gotta say, your property is beautiful."

"I enjoy landscaping. When my husband and I lived in Queens, it was all concrete, blacktop, and patches of grass… I'm in another world when I'm home now."

Billy's cell phone rings and he answers, "What's the word?"

Nutsy stands outside the hospital and replies, "He flatlined."

Billy nervously stands up and replies, "What!"

"He's alright. He pulled through."

"He's conscious?"

"Yeah, finally."

"Alright, I'll be there in a little while."

"What's that noise in the background?" Nutsy curiously asks.

"I'm close to the roundabout fountain. I'll see you soon."
Billy doesn't want to tell Nutsy where he is and hangs up.

An older lady is walking her dog through the wooded area
where Leo had dumped Vito's body. Her dog is barking
relentlessly. "Be quiet," the lady whispers.

Her dog can't help itself and continues barking away while
pulling her toward the pile of leaves Vito is lying under.
The dog pauses by the pile and continues barking. "Come
on, let's go." The lady tugs her dog away.

Munchie enters Ladro's hospital room and asks, "What
the hell happened?"

"I don't know. I didn't see the person." Ladro doesn't want
Blackie to know who it was since he wants to take care
of Vito on his own. He's concerned Blackie will retaliate
before he gets out.

"I heard you went under this morning?"

"Yeah, I went to a beautiful place." Ladro can't get the thought of the sports park out of his mind. "A lot nicer than this fucking city, trust me."

Munchie says to Blackie, "He seems like his normal self to me. Can I talk to him for a minute?"

Blackie nods and heads into the hallway.

Munchie asks Ladro, "Could you please talk to Nutsy about this bet? I'm a loser either way."

"Not really. I would've kept the whole fucking thing and gave you back shit. Nutsy's at least giving you the benefit of the doubt."

"Keeping the money if I lose and returning my wager if I win, I wouldn't call for my benefit."

"You screwed up, Munchie. The only reason Nutsy is even giving you a chance, is because you keep us alive."

"You know it's not all my money though."

"Just pray the over hits today. Then you got nothing to worry about."

"No, just a small fortune of my own money that I'll lose."

"How many fucking times has Nutsy told you to calm down and stop betting, ha?"

"A lot."

"You bet your ass a lot. Just be glad it's him and not me. I would've tossed you down the steps headfirst trying some bullshit like that."

Blackie enters the room with a cup of coffee and asks, "You done yet?"

The nurse enters the room and notices Munchie so she turns and walks out. If she only knew what their conversation was about.

Blackie asks, "How is he?"

"He seems perfectly fine to me," Munchie replies and heads out.

Blackie asks, "What's wrong with him?"

"Who knows, maybe he couldn't keep up with Belinda this morning... hey, how about you hop up here."

Nutsy overhears Ladro's comment while entering the room and sarcastically says, "I guess he's alright."

Ladro laughs and asks, "Who owns that dump anyway?"

"I don't know. It could be the county by now."

Blackie asks, "What dump? That field Nutsy always stares at?"

As Ladro nods yes, Blackie asks, "Why, what about it?"

Ladro replies, "It's gonna be spectacular, that's what."

Blackie glances toward Nutsy and asks, "What's he talking about?"

"Who the fuck knows, he's your husband, isn't he?"

CHAPTER 3

Kathy stands by her six-burner kitchen stove flipping pancakes. Eight pancakes are already stacked on a plate sitting on the granite counter. Sammy, N-J, and Carmela sit by the island having breakfast while in a conversation.

Kathy flips the last one on top of the stack and moves toward the island with the plate and says, "This will make fifteen, total. I feel like I'm feeding a football team."

N-J replies, "I can't wait for today's game. I'm gonna show Papa I'm right."

"Right about what?" Sammy asks.

"I told him the over was going to hit later."

Kathy interjects, "I told you, I don't want you thinking about gambling."

Carmela chimes in, "Ah, so what… let him have fun."

"Your son doesn't look like he's having fun these days."

"It pays the bills, doesn't it?" Carmela is old school and a buck is a buck to her since money was hard to come by after Nutsy's father had passed away.

A car horn beeps outside and Sammy quickly stands up. Kathy asks her, "Where are you going?"

"It's probably Bono. We're going to The Plains."

"For what?"

"He signed up for a karate lesson and asked if I'd come to watch."

"Does your father know about this?"

"He left early. I didn't see him this morning."

"You should tell –"

Carmela buts in, "Let her go and have fun with that nice young boy."

"Can I come?" N-J asks.

Kathy replies, "Your father was going to ask if you wanted to come to the club with us for the fundraiser later."

"The place with the beach?"

"Yeah, you remember that place, right?"

"Absolutely," N-J excitedly replies.

Presto drives on the Hutch heading north with his wife, son, and daughter. His son, age 16, finished a travel baseball game earlier in the morning close to Jones Beach and got knocked out of the weekend tournament sooner than planned.

They have been sitting in horrendous traffic in the Bronx area and everyone is getting fidgety. His wife says with an annoyed tone, "I don't understand why there's always traffic here."

His daughter says from the backseat, "Dad, I have to go to the bathroom."

Presto replies, "I got an idea. How about we stop off where I grew up, get something to eat, and find a bathroom."

"How far is it from here?" His daughter asks.

"The next town up."

The phone rings through the Bluetooth and Presto answers, "Hello."

"Any word yet on the claim? My neighbor keeps busting my balls," Squalo asks while staring at his warped, wood floor.

Presto's wife gives him a look and rolls her eyes while Squalo continues on, "I found out he's a litigation attorney. It's just my fucking luck."

Presto's wife nods toward the back seat since she's concerned about the kids hearing the conversation. Presto picks up the phone so his kids can't hear through the Bluetooth anymore and says, "A cracked tank isn't covered."

"I thought you were taking care of it?"

"How do I take care of that, Squalo? It is what it is."

Squalo has enough of the back and forth and replies, "No wonder the insurance companies have all the fucking money.

They take in and never pay out. And they call the bookies crooks?"

Presto rolls his eyes at his wife and replies, "Yeah, I'm sorry. There's not too much I can do."

"I bet your father would've figured something out." Squalo hangs up and mumbles, "Yeah, some fucking insurance agent. He can't hold his father's jock strap."

Presto hangs up from the call and his son asks, "Dad, who's that guy?"

"An old family friend and client."

"He sounds like a mafia guy or someone like that."

As Presto laughs, his wife cuts in the conversation, "Your father doesn't deal with people like that."

Their daughter chimes in, "You could've fooled me. I saw scenes from the Godfather and he sounds like that big guy in it."

"When did you see it?" Presto asks.

"I don't know, one day at my friend's house… are we almost there? I really have to go."

"Soon, squeeze harder," Presto replies.

Ladro's room is now packed with family and guests. The nurse keeps asking people to leave but more keep on piling in. Kathy decides to bring N-J and Carmela and they all wait by the door since the room is too crowded.

Nutsy says to Kathy, "I'll be right back. I gotta stop by the shop."

When Nutsy starts to leave, N-J asks him, "Dad, I'm coming later, right?"

"If ya wanna."

"Of course. I can skip rocks on the beach."

Nutsy nods and heads down the hallway.

Belinda is in a heated argument with Leo in her office at the body shop, or let's just say, Leo's new office. Belinda is not ready to give it all up to Leo just yet, after hearing what her next role would be.

Leo decided that Belinda would be calling on local dealerships that use them for their shop's services. Leo wants her to convince the service agents to cut the sunroof lines that drain out of the bottom of the car. This could cause the car to flood and hopefully create additional work for the shop.

Leo also wants her to convince Munchie to sign off on social security claim forms so his workers could get paid by the government and not from the shop's revenue.

Belinda wants no part of it and in so many words told Leo to screw off. Leo knows she cares for Munchie from their earlier conversations and is using that against her to get what he wants. After a few minutes of their bickering,

Leo has enough and says, "It's pretty simple. He either agrees or –"

"Or what?" Belinda asks with a serious tone.

"I'm sure you can figure it out."

"You know something. You never learned a thing. You should've rotted in that jail."

"Well, I'm here, so –"

"You're no different from dad. You're both connivers and no good."

"You're wrong. I'm worse and don't forget that… I want your shit out by tomorrow."

The door flies open and Nutsy charges in and asks, "Where the fuck is he?"

"Who the hell said you can come in here?" Leo asks.

"I'm not gonna ask again."

Belinda replies, "If you're referring to Vito, he never showed up this morning."

So Nutsy just stares them down and replies, "You let me know when that punk shows his face." Nutsy heads toward the door.

"Yeah, we'll let you know right away," Leo sarcastically replies.

As Nutsy turns and stares at Leo for a moment, Belinda says, "I heard he wasn't the one who jabbed your daughter."

"I ain't here for that."

"For what then?" Belinda asks.

Nutsy nods toward Leo and replies, "Ask this asshole. He'll tell ya." Nutsy storms out.

Belinda asks Leo, "What's he talking about?"

"How am I supposed to know? I just got out." The last thing Leo would ever do is admit the truth, even to his own sister.

Presto and his family finally made it off the Hutch Parkway and are sitting in Maddie's Tavern in the north end of the city. The tavern is pub style with dark wood tables and booths along the perimeter. Scuffed up wood floors are throughout with a few flat screen TVs bolted on the walls.

Presto's daughter finally made it to the bathroom and has taken a seat at the table with the rest of the family after snooping around. "Dad, this place has a rooftop?"

"Yeah, it must be new. I haven't been down here in years."

"Why does everyone talk like they're from Brooklyn down here?" Presto's son asks.

As Presto laughs, Nutsy enters through the front door and pauses by the bar off to the side of the room. He's looking for one of the workers who dropped six hundred last week on the baseball playoffs. Nutsy asks the bartender, "Timmy in yet?"

"He took off today, Nutsy," the bartender replies.

"Ya tell him to call me when ya see him."

Presto's searching for extra napkins, so he heads toward the bar and is ready to ask the bartender when Nutsy turns and they collide. At first, they both pause to see who excuses themselves but then Presto recognizes Nutsy. "Is that you, Nuccio?"

Nutsy stares trying to figure out who he is and replies, "Don't tell me this is Presto?"

"I don't believe it. I haven't seen you in thirty years."

They hug and Nutsy asks, "I heard ya moved up the line years ago. What brings ya down here?"

"My kid played a travel baseball game on the island today so I decided to show them the old neighborhood. I can't believe how much has changed down here."

"Yeah, some good and some bad… is that your son with the uniform on?" Nutsy nods toward Presto's table.

"Yeah, come on over. Let me introduce you."

They both walk back to the table and Presto says, "This is my wife, Tammy. My son, Michael, and daughter, Nicole… this is an old neighborhood friend, Nuccio."

Nutsy exchanges a handshake with all of them and asks Michael, "So did ya win, or what?"

Michael replies, "No, we lost five to one."

Presto chimes in, "Nuccio, they can't hit like we did. I tell him all the time to keep his head down on the ball, but do you –"

Tammy cuts him off, "Alright, let's not get into this here." She's been hearing this topic the whole way home.

As Nutsy and Presto catch eyes, Nutsy laughs and curiously asks, "You said it was a travel baseball game. What's that?"

"You never heard of travel baseball?"

"Here and there."

"Take a seat. You have to hear about this racket."

"I don't have that much time."

"Ten minutes. I haven't seen you in years." So, Presto slides over a chair from another table and Nutsy takes a seat.

"How come you're on the island playing?" Nutsy asks.

"Oh shit, Nuccio, you would love it. They have complexes where over a hundred teams play ball all weekend… remember how we played at Brink Park? Picture that a hundred times over."

"I'm not following ya."

"Alright, check this out. Today they have independent teams and families pay to play at tournaments. Some teams travel up and down the coast. It's insane."

"Let me get this right. You pay for your son to play on his team and travel around just to play games?"

"That's right and it isn't cheap. Trust me."

"No it's not." Tammy says.

"Who would do that?" Nutsy curiously asks. He can't comprehend the idea.

"Families pay to play today, Nuccio. It's nothing like when we played… they got three-hundred dollar bats, two – hundred dollar –"

"What?!"

"Yeah, this is what I'm saying. It's a bigger racket than the numbers."

"Nutsy laughs and asks, "You still in insurance?"

"Yeah, I'll tell you, I'd love to get out though. The business is changing."

"Tell me about it." Nutsy stands up and says, "It was a pleasure to meet you all. I gotta go." Nutsy exchanges a handshake with everyone and then says, "Presto, let's keep in touch. Ya got me puzzled with this travel stuff."

"Of course." So Presto whips out a business card from his pants pocket and hands it off to Nutsy. Nutsy slips it in his jacket pocket and says, "Good to see ya again, Presto. It looks like livin' in the sticks is agreeing with ya."

Nutsy heads toward the bar. He places a hundred-dollar bill on the wood counter and says to the bartender, "Pay for their lunch and give the rest to the waitress. I haven't seen this guy in decades."

Michael curiously watches Nutsy leave the tavern and asks, "Who was that, dad?"

"An old friend I grew up with."

Nicole says, "Now that guy looks like a Mafioso."

Tammy asks, "Is that the guy you said hit the longest ball you ever saw anyone hit?"

"Yup... I was a great hitter, but that guy?"

Michael's eyes roll. "Here we go again with the hitting."

"Let me tell you something. You and your team couldn't hold a candle to me and my friends at the plate years back."

"I know, dad, and you all walked five miles in the snow to get to school," Michael sarcastically replies.

"You're damn right we did, and to work."

CHAPTER 4

Sammy and Bono are at the karate class Bono signed up for. It's a typical karate school with a large room and wood floors. Most areas have thick black mats covering the floor and floor to ceiling mirrors on the walls.

While Bono stands with an instructor in the middle of the room, Sammy sits off to the side watching. She figures if she could pick up additional tips, it's worth sitting here for a half hour. Even if she didn't, she's just glad to spend time with Bono since their friendship seems to be heading in a different direction.

The instructor keeps peeking over toward Sammy. She's intrigued by the shape Sammy's in and is impressed by her rounded shoulders being displayed by her tight T-shirt.

Although Bono is in decent shape, he doesn't have the thick, sturdy appearance that Sammy has. The instructor asks Bono, "Is that your girlfriend over there?"

"Well... I don't know." Bono has no idea how to respond to the instructor's question, but he knows he cares for Sammy.

"She seems like she's in decent shape. Does she work out?" Although the instructor is working with Bono, she loves the idea of training teenage girls.

"She trains every week with her aunt."

"They lift weights?"

"Nah… they do this, karate."

"Oh, her aunt's an instructor?"

"No, she just knows it and I heard she's great."

So the instructor asks Sammy, "Excuse me, Miss, you're learning karate?"

"Well, somewhat, I just work out with my aunt in her basement," Sammy replies.

"What's her name?"

"Maria Tisi."

The instructor ponders it over for a moment and replies, "No, her name doesn't sound familiar. Is she married?"

"Yeah, her maiden name is mine, Gento."

The instructor's eyes open wide and she asks, "Your aunt is Maria Gento?"

"Yeah, you know her?"

"We were in the same training class years ago. I couldn't believe how good she was."

"Well, she still is."

The instructor glances toward Bono and asks, "Would you mind if she joins us? It's no extra charge." The instructor is curious to see what Blackie has taught Sammy.

"No, of course not," Bono replies.

"It's okay. I'm just here to watch," Sammy says.

Bono replies, "Come on, Sammy, join us. You've helped me all this time."

So Sammy stands up and walks over. She loves the idea of joining and learning anything she can.

Blackie stops back at her house and slips a pistol holster down the front of her leather pants. She snaps a full magazine into the handle of the pistol and slides it into the holster. She puts a jacket on and heads out of the house.

Blackie presses a button on her dashboard and revs the engine of her car. She slams on the gas and her car peels out down the street. Her phone rings and Nutsy is on the other end while driving back to the hospital. "How is he?"

Blackie replies, "I had to stop back home for a minute. I'll be there in ten. I just gotta stop off somewhere."

"Where?"

"Are you my mother now?"

"Don't do anything stupid. I'm stopping by later to pick up the pistol."

Blackie hangs up without responding and hits the gas.

Nutsy hangs up from the call and mumbles, "This fuckin' girl's gonna drive me nuts."

About five minutes later, Blackie pulls up in front of Belinda's body shop and steps out of the car. She enters the lobby and quickly moves toward the office door without acknowledging the secretary. The secretary notices Blackie and says, "They're in a meeting."

Blackie totally ignores her comment and kicks open the door. Belinda and Leo are in the throes of another heated argument, so the bang from the door slamming against the wall startles them. "Who did it?" Blackie asks.

"Did what?" Belinda asks.

"Put Ladro in the hospital, that's what."

Leo chimes in, "Now that's the Blackie I remember busting doors down, taking no shit from anyone."

"How about, I bust your fucking head open?"

So Leo laughs like the cocky man he is while Blackie continues on with a stern tone, "I'm not gonna ask again."

Belinda asks, "What happened to Ladro?" She has no clue what transpired last night.

Leo cuts in, "Your brother was just here asking the same bullshit. You're both barking up the wrong tree."

Blackie and Leo stare for a moment and then Leo sarcastically says, "I'm impressed. You still got it all. Even your ass still looks good."

Belinda cuts in since she knows this conversation can turn ugly quickly from her brother's comment. "If I hear anything, I'll let you know."

"You ain't telling this wench a thing, you hear me?" Leo threatens Belinda.

So Blackie has heard enough and yanks out the pistol from inside her pants. Leo laughs and sarcastically asks, "Oh, so now you're gonna shoot us?"

"No, only you." Blackie points the pistol down toward Leo's feet and pulls on the trigger. BANG! After grazing Leo's foot, the bullet ricochets off the floor and sticks into a wall. Leo drops to the ground clutching his foot and yells out, "You bitch!"

"You should know I don't bluff," Blackie replies as she moves toward the door. "I just skinned you anyway. Next time it will be right down the center." Blackie storms out and yanks the door shut.

Leo lies on the ground clutching his foot in pain. Belinda can't believe what Blackie had done and asks, "Should I call an ambulance?"

Leo removes his shoe and sock and a bloody gash runs across the side of his foot. He shakes his head no with a pissed off look and replies, "Take me to your boyfriend."

CHAPTER 5

Nutsy is standing next to Ladro's bed. Ladro still can't get the visions of the sports park out of his mind and keeps on bringing them up. Nutsy, however, keeps on blowing him off since he currently has other things racing through his mind.

Papo enters the room and says, "I never doubted you, Ladro." He exchanges a handshake with Ladro and then asks Nutsy, "Can I have a word with you in private?"

Nutsy nods and heads out of the room and they both pause by a quiet area in the hallway. "What's up?" Nutsy asks.

"Listen, I know I keep bringing this up, but my brother is getting nervous. He wants to pull his family in."

"Papo, we spoke about this. We still don't know a hundred percent who sent him."

"It's not even about last night. This derelict getting out is not sitting right with him."

"Let it play out first. I'm not jumping to any conclusions."

"You remember our pact from that night, right?"

Nutsy stares into Papo's eyes. He knows exactly where he's heading with this and hesitantly replies, "I remember. Things are a little different today though."

"A pact is a pact, isn't it?"

So Nutsy turns his head while deep in thought. He knows he gave his word years back, but his thoughts are different today since he has a family to worry about. He truly believes Sammy could take care of herself if need be, but it's N-J that troubles him. He knows he needs to be around as long as possible since its unlikely N-J will ever have a family of his own to take care of him.

Nutsy's in a tough spot and he knows it. He still carries around the rough reputation from the past, and he has to, but he feels he needs to be smarter about how he handles things for his family's future. He tries to not let anyone know his thoughts regarding N-J since most would take it as a weakness, and some, like Squalo, already do.

This city is full of opportunists and a pact is a pact, but being around for N-J is on the top of Nutsy's list. So Nutsy just nods to acknowledge Papo.

"Alright… on a different note, what's this shit about a baseball complex you were mentioning?" Papo asks.

"We'll talk another time. I'm still trying to figure it out."

"Just so you know, there's no money in it. I already looked into building one. It's the fastest way to bankruptcy."

"It ain't about the money for me."

"The money is number one, Nutsy. Without that, investors won't even listen."

"I know. That's the part I still have to figure out. For me, it's for a different cause, but I know I gotta make them happy."

"What different cause could there be besides money?"

Blackie heads down the hallway and notices Nutsy and Papo in the corner having their discussion. She continues passed them without acknowledging either one and Papo says to Nutsy, "She looks pissed."

"Yeah, what else is new?"

Blackie enters Ladro's room and Ladro asks, "Where were you?"

"I had to take care of a few things."

"Like what?"

"Like it's none of your business."

Leo hobbles into one of Munchie's examining rooms still in tremendous pain. Belinda follows with an annoyed look and asks, "Why did you have to say that to her?"

Leo ignores her question and looks away. Belinda shakes her head and peeks out from one of the windows and hesitantly asks, "You still like her, don't you?"

"What are you asking me?"

"You know exactly what I'm asking. You always had a thing for her."

"She's a fucking bitch, that's what she is."

"Yeah sure... you just couldn't ever win her over."

"I never wanted her. If I did, she would've been mine."

Belinda just laughs at Leo's response while Munchie enters the room and closes the door. "What's going on?"

Leo removes his sock and says, "I cut my foot on a piece of metal in the shop."

Munchie takes a glimpse and peeks toward Belinda who is watching with an annoyed look. Munchie knows there is more to this than it appears. He's uncertain if he should question Leo, so Munchie continues to examine Leo's foot without a word.

Belinda gazes out of the window again. Munchie can tell by Belinda's demeanor that she is not thrilled with whatever had happened. "So, how did this happen?" Munchie nonchalantly asks.

"Some asshole left a metal bar on the floor and I tripped over it."

Munchie sighs and glances toward Belinda again. Leo can sense his hesitation and becomes firmer with his response. "You look like you don't believe my answer."

Munchie doesn't want to upset Leo any further. He can tell whatever happened has pissed Leo off, so he decides to go along with it. "Yeah, I believe you. You might need some stitches."

"Well, whatever I need, fix it. I gotta make this fundraiser later."

"You'll have to stay off this for a while."

"Give me crutches for the day."

Belinda drives back to the shop with Leo. Leo wants to continue their conversation from before and asks, "So what's this bullshit about me liking Blackie?"

Belinda laughs and replies, "It was clear then and it's clear now."

"What the hell are you talking about?"

"Let me ask YOU something. If a worker shot you in the foot, what would you do?"

"He'd be fish food in the Hudson."

"That's exactly my point."

Ladro seems to be more alert and responsive. Although he still feels tremendous pain on the side of his head, his spirits are rising and he's becoming his sarcastic self again. Nutsy sips from a coffee container while Ladro asks him, "You still going to the fundraiser?"

Nutsy nods yes and takes another sip.

"You tell those pricks the thief is good to go."

Nutsy just nods and doesn't reply.

"What's wrong with you?" Ladro curiously asks.

"Ya never gonna believe who I ran into before."

"Who?"

"Ya remember Presto?"

"Of course, we went to the Hamptons with him a few weekends… it was when he got the house with like, ten other guys… who's that other guy he hung around with all the time?"

"He hung around with a lot of guys. He was like fuckin' shit back then, all over the place."

"Ladro laughs and replies, "Yeah, I know what you mean, we all were. I thought he moved up to cow country. What the hell was he doing down here?"

"He was on his way back from his son's baseball game."

"Down here?"

"Yeah, travel baseball… ya ever hear about this shit?"

"A little… I think they're all fucking nuts. Who wants to travel all over to play a game?"

"He said it's bigger than we know. It's what all the families do now."

"Well, I guess with me having no kids and N-J not playing, we haven't been in that circle."

So Nutsy turns away deep in thought. He's curious to know if this travel program has been the missing link to the puzzle of his dream. Although the travel concept has been around, not many in his city have been exposed to it.

"What are you thinking?" Ladro curiously asks.

"Nothing."

"I know that look very well."

Nutsy heads home in his car to get ready for the fundraiser. He curiously peeks at Presto's business card and decides to call him.

Presto is now sitting on his paver patio in his wooded backyard having a beer and answers his cell phone, "Hello."

While Nutsy turns down his street, he says, "I'm lookin' for Presto."

"Yeah, who's this?"

"Nuccio Gento."

"Hey, that was fast. It's me."

"Yeah, listen… ya got me curious about this travel baseball shit."

"I know you were always a baseball guy. You'd love it, Nuccio. I'm surprised you never got involved with it with your son."

So Nutsy stays silent for a minute. "Nuccio, you still there?" Presto asks.

"Yeah, I'm here… my son doesn't live with me."

"Oh, my apologies, I didn't realize you got divorced."

"I didn't… he has autism and lives somewhere else."

"Oh, I had no idea… sorry about that."

"No need to apologize, he's a good son… listen… when can we talk about this?"

"I'm free now if you want."

"I can't. I gotta get ready for a city fundraiser. I'm running late as it is."

"I'll tell you what. If you don't mind taking a trip this Thursday, my son's team is playing in Grange to start off a Columbus weekend tournament."

"Grange? Where the hell is that?"

Presto laughs and replies, "The next town over from mine. There's a brand new baseball complex there. You can see exactly what I'm talking about."

"I'll call ya during the week and let ya know."

"You call me anytime, old friend."

"Hey, it's good to hear your voice again. I always enjoyed your company, Presto." Nutsy hangs up.

Presto hangs up from the call and Tammy asks while taking a seat at the patio table, "Who was that?"

"That guy I introduced you to at the tavern."

"Who, that hitman looking guy?"

"He's not a hitman. He's just a bookie from the old neighborhood."

"I don't want you getting involved with any of that crap."

"He's asking me about travel baseball, that's it."

"Yeah, I know those guys. That's how it all starts out."

"It's just nice to hear from old friends once in a while instead of listening to crickets and watching groundhogs eat my tomatoes." A lawnmower fires up across the street. "And lawnmowers."

"Still, you moved up here to get away from all that, didn't you?"

"My old neighborhood is a place that will always be in my blood… it's hard to explain."

Nutsy wanders into his bedroom. He moves toward his closet and removes a fresh shirt from a hanger and slips it on.

Kathy roams in and asks, "We're still bringing N-J, right?"

"Yeah, does he still wanna come?"

"Are you kidding me? All he talks about is feeding the ducks."

"N-J!" Nutsy yells out.

From the other room, N-J replies, "Yeah, Papa?"

"Get ready, we're leaving soon."

"I've been ready."

Kathy says, "You know your son, he doesn't wait for the last minute like you do."

"I was busy."

CHAPTER 6

Belo and Linda enter Ladro's hospital room and say hello to a few visitors. They both give Blackie a kiss and then shake hands with Ladro.

Linda sits down next to Blackie and says, "I'm so sorry, Blackie."

"He's getting better. It's all that matters right now."

Belo starts to ask Ladro about the safe and Ladro cuts him off with an annoyed tone, "I told you at the party, it wasn't me who hit it."

"Ladro, I had over a hundred and eighty grand in there."

"You ain't the only one, now were you?"

"Not many people knew about that money and could've pulled it off," Belo replies insinuating it had to be Ladro.

"Yeah well, with my leg and shit, how could you even question me?"

Linda says to Blackie, "I just hope none of this changes my relationship with you and Kathy."

"Linda, we've always liked you and considered you a friend. We can't help if our asshole husbands wanna act like children."

Belo says to Ladro, "You know Nutsy's busting my balls, right?"

As Ladro laughs at the comment, Belo continues on, "It's not funny, Ladro. I told him a thousand times I'm sorry, but he keeps on blowing me off like I'm a child... I don't wanna side with Leo, but Nutsy's not giving me a choice."

"So go independent then."

"Independent? This ain't a political party."

"Ah, in a way it is."

"He listens to you... you need to talk to him."

"Nutsy listens but he makes his own decisions."

"You can sway him though. I've seen you do it before."

"Don't kid yourself. It's only after his mind has already been made up."

Squalo stands with the building manager in his apartment while staring at his warped, wood floor and says, "You tell that asshole downstairs I ain't paying for shit. It's gonna cost me enough to tear this all up."

"That's not the point. It was your tank that caused their damage downstairs. My hands are tied, Squalo."

"Tell him to fucking sue me then because I ain't paying out of pocket for it."

Nutsy brushes his hair in his bathroom, then heads into his bedroom and puts on his sports jacket. Sammy peeks in the room and asks, "Dad, how many tables did you get?"

"I don't know, three, four, why?"

"Can my friend come?"

"What friend is this now?"

"My same friend, Bono."

"Come in for a minute."

Sammy enters Nutsy's bedroom and he asks, "What's the deal with this kid? And don't tell me you're just friends."

"Well, we are."

"I noticed ya two gettin' a little giddy at the party. And why was he talkin' to Belo?"

"He's his uncle."

"His what?!"

"His uncle. Didn't mom tell you?"

"She knows?"

"Yeah, for a while now."

"Kathy!" Nutsy yells out.

Kathy replies from the kitchen downstairs, "What?!"

"I need ya up here for a minute."

Sammy turns to leave the room and Nutsy says, "Wait here a minute."

Sammy rolls her eyes and waits. About thirty seconds later, Kathy roams in and asks, "What is it?"

Nutsy asks, "Did ya know that kid is Belo's nephew?"

"What kid?" Kathy doesn't want to commit she knows.

"The kid ya didn't tell me about, that's who."

"I still don't know —"

Sammy cuts in, "I already told him, ma."

Kathy attempts to play it off and replies, "Oh, him. I told you already the other day."

"Ya didn't tell me shit."

"You just don't listen when I speak."

"Trust me, THAT, I woulda heard."

"You have selective hearing."

"Yeah sure, it seems whenever I catch ya in a lie, ya already told me about it."

"Well, I did. You should listen more often." Kathy walks out.

While Nutsy stares at Sammy, she just shrugs it off and Nutsy says, "So let me get back to my original question. What's the deal with you two?"

"I don't even know right now myself… can he come or not?"

Nutsy reluctantly nods yes and replies, "He can take Uncle Larry's seat."

"And what, sit right next to you?"

"That's right."

"Nothing's ever easy with you."

"Now ya know how I feel."

Sammy leaves the bedroom and Nutsy mumbles to himself, "Yeah, put these shoes on for a day."

Sammy replies from the hallway, "I heard that."

"Ya got elephant ears like your mother."

"At least we both listen," Sammy sarcastically replies.

Nutsy sarcastically replies, "Yeah sure, ya both listen alright."

After finishing getting ready, Nutsy heads downstairs and passes Kathy in the foyer and asks, "What's her deal with this kid?"

"Will you stop calling him a kid. He's eighteen."

"Oh, I'm sorry. He probably hasn't paid a bill like your daughter yet, but he's an adult… I asked ya, what's going on?"

"How do I know?"

"You're her mother, aren't ya?"

"They're just good friends."

"It didn't look that way to me at N-J's party."

"Nutsy, stop it, will you. He's a nice boy... and he's gay so you have nothing to worry about."

"They're the ones ya have to worry about. It's probably just a front."

Kathy sighs and replies, "You really have a warped mind, I gotta say."

"Yeah I know, until I'm right... I can't wait to find out what else ya haven't told me." Nutsy heads toward the front door. "I'm gonna stop by the hospital first. I'll see ya all there."

Nutsy wanders into Ladro's room and notices him sitting up in bed. "Ya lookin' better."

"I'm coming today to the fundraiser."

"No ya ain't."

"I gotta get the fuck outta this place. All I hear are people moaning and beeps all day."

Nutsy laughs and replies, "Yeah, I'm sure... if you're out by then, you can take a ride with me up to Grange."

"Jeez, that's all the way up there."

"Ya heard of it?"

"Yeah, my cousin Ralphie moved up there. I think all he does is yank his chain all day... why there?"

"There's a baseball complex I wanna check out."

"Ah… I was right before, wasn't I?"

"You're hot, that's all I'm sayin' right now."

"Yeah sure, when did you ever say anything anyway?"

Nutsy just shrugs off the question.

Ladro continues, "Yeah, I ain't gonna lie… I'm lying in here wondering what I've really accomplished in life… absolutely nothing."

"Ya just made the biggest score of your life."

"So what? In the end, I'm still a criminal."

"You? How about me? I'm still bookin' the same teaser bets since I'm twenty… and dealin' with the same pricks who've been tryin' to screw me over since day one."

"I know you don't wanna commit, but we gotta chase this dream of yours. Don't you wanna leave knowing you did something good with your life?"

"It's not that I don't wanna commit."

"No? What is it then?"

"Just get better, alright… I need ya back in the shop as soon as possible." Nutsy turns and walks away.

"Hey!" Ladro yells out. Nutsy turns back and nods.

"Remember this. Regret of never trying will cut deeper than giving it a shot. There's a reason you keep staring at that dump… that dream is buried in you whether you like it or not."

"I'm fifty and I only got one shot to make it work. Until the missing link is figured out, it's only a passing thought, not a dream, Ladro. Get some rest." Nutsy walks out.

Ladro yells out, "Rest? Fuck that, I gotta get the hell outta here!"

CHAPTER 7

Nutsy drives toward a catering hall located on the Long Island Sound in New Row. It's on the grounds of a beach club that the political party has been using for their fundraisers. In fact, one of the top party contributors is the manager of the place and Billy knows him well.

Nutsy pulls in front of a large colonial style house that has been converted into a catering hall. He steps out of the car with cash in his hand then slips the valet worker a twenty and says, "Park it where I won't get blocked in. I might wanna leave early."

"Of course, Mr. Gento. Where's Mr. Tisi today?" The valet worker has been there for years and knows them both well.

"He took a fall the other night. You know us old folks." Nutsy laughs and enters the hall.

Billy is in the back room with Marcus and Staci figuring out the profit from today's ticket sales. "Not bad," Billy says while glancing at the bottom of a piece of paper.

"When's Nutsy going to join us?" Staci asks. She always adored Nutsy since their high school years. In fact, she always had a crush on him but never let anyone know except her father.

Her father was the mayor at the time and Billy ran the political party, so her father always told her never to let anyone know. She knew down deep inside it was a longshot to ever have a relationship with Nutsy since he was involved with illegal activities. Besides, he was of Italian decent and she was African American with deep political ties. He was head over heels about Kathy anyway, and Staci always knew it, so her thoughts just remained between herself and her father.

Billy replies, "You've known him for years, Staci. You got a better shot of trying to sell him ice pops in the winter."

While Staci laughs, Marcus asks, "What's this rumor about Ladro getting clubbed over the head?"

"We're still trying to figure it out."

"Do you think it has anything to do with Leo getting out?"

"We're not sure."

Katy, a long-time volunteer, has been running a soup kitchen on the southside of town. She has known Nutsy for years since they went to high school together and have remained friendly ever since. When the kitchen needs additional funding, which it frequently does, Nutsy is always one of her first visits. So, she figures today would be a great time to ask him for a donation since they are already attending a fundraiser. After chatting and catching up with family stories, Nutsy says, "I give ya credit, Katy, you've been at it for years and haven't given up."

"I can't, Nutsy, I know how important it is for some people... it's all they have."

Nutsy smiles and replies, "You and your family have always had big hearts, never lose it, Katy. Come by my bar next week."

"We both have big hearts, Nutsy. We just show it in different ways."

Donnola sits in the passenger seat of an FBI agent's car. A few years back he was approached by the Feds regarding his operation and they made Donnola a deal. The Feds believe Donnola's a follower and weak inside, so they've been using him for information or he's looking at jail time, so they say.

Donnola has also been feeding them information about Nutsy's lucrative sports betting operation. As of now, the only thing saving Nutsy is Sista Bar and Grill since it's totally legit and successful.

Billy made sure Nutsy invested in a few legit operations years back and they have been paying off and keeping him from getting busted. Nutsy reports the proceeds from the legal operations and sprinkles some of his bookmaking profits through them. Since the majority of his ventures deal with cash, it's easy for him to bury money.

Donnola was always resentful of Nutsy from their childhood. Nutsy has always gotten the respect from the majority of his friends, whereas Donnola was always picked on and looked down upon.

It wasn't any of Nutsy's doing since Nutsy was never the type of person to pick on anyone, but it always made Donnola jealous of the notoriety Nutsy received. In the end, they are all criminals to some degree, but Nutsy was treated like a celebrity and very well respected.

"See what you can find out today... and especially about Leo and what he's up to," the FBI agent says.

Donnola nods yes in agreement and gets out of the car.

Binky, an old school Bronx bookie, happens to be passing by after visiting a friend at his boat club nearby. He notices Donnola closing the door of the marked car and catches eyes with the FBI agent. The agent quickly ducks his head to avoid Binky from noticing him, but he was too late. He's the same agent who used to give Binky a hard time years back until Binky had to set him straight.

Binky has deep ties to big players from downtown Manhattan. The agent was barking up the wrong tree and turned his attention to Donnola since he's a loner and a known weasel.

Nutsy stands at the bar with a few city players and some local friends. Many are clients of Nutsy's and they know he would never say anything to anyone. This has always helped Nutsy's business stay successful since the bettors in his city know their habits are safe with him.

Billy approaches Nutsy at the bar and asks, "Where's the crew?"

"They should be here soon."

"Can I have a word with you?"

Nutsy nods yes and they head toward a corner of the large open room. Billy asks, "What's the total booked on the game today?" Billy has been concerned about this game all week.

"Close to six."

"Jesus Christ! Is it all one way?"

"Yeah, pretty much on the under."

Billy turns his head with a nervous look and then asks, "How come you don't seem to be worried about it?"

"It will be what it will be, Billy."

So Billy stares into Nutsy's eyes. He gets a feeling like there's more to Nutsy's reasoning and asks, "Is there anything I need to be concerned about?"

"Yeah, don't drink too much today. Come on, everything will work out."

While Nutsy heads back to the bar, Billy just stares. He knows Nutsy is up to something and doesn't like the fact he's not aware of it since Billy always wants to be one step ahead of everyone else.

While standing at the bar, Nutsy's cell phone rings and he answers, "What's up?"

Blackie's driving toward the catering hall and asks, "Do you have an extra seat?"

"For who?"

"Me."

"I don't think ya comin' to the fundraiser, is a good idea."

"Why, I can't support my city?"

"Come on, we all know that's not –"

"I just asked if you have an extra ticket. I don't need a fucking lecture."

Nutsy sighs and hesitantly replies, "Yeah, I do. I don't want –"

Blackie hangs up before Nutsy finishes and slams on the gas.

Nutsy mumbles to himself, "After all these years, she's still drivin' me nuts."

So Nutsy dials Ladro at the hospital. Ladro fumbles around the sheets searching for his cell phone. "Where the fuck is this thing?" Ladro finally finds the phone between the sheets and answers, "Yeah?"

Nutsy stands by the bar and says, "Do me a favor, call your wife and tell her coming today is a bad idea."

"How do you know she's going?"

"She just asked me for a ticket."

"Alright, I'll call you right back."

Ladro hangs up from the call and presses Blackie's number. Blackie continues to drive toward the catering hall and answers her phone through the car's Bluetooth, "How it's going?"

"I need you at the hospital."

"Why?"

"I just do."

"I have to stop off somewhere first."

"Don't go to the fundraiser."

"What did Nutsy put you up to this? I'm going." Blackie hangs up and hits the gas.

Billy and the Mayor of the city head toward Nutsy. She is the first female mayor and extremely proud of it. She's well aware of Nutsy's operation but has also respected Billy and Nutsy for many years and turns a blind eye. Nutsy notices the both of them approaching and says, "Mayor, it's always a pleasure to be a part of this."

So the mayor extends her hand out for a handshake and replies, "Nuccio, thank you again for the generous donation. I know I can always count on you."

"Hey, ya know me. If I like ya, ya have my backin' one hundred percent."

The mayor smiles and replies, "So, Billy mentioned to me you have your eye on the sports park for some reason."

Nutsy knows Billy's trying to push the situation along and replies, "Ah... I just go there to reminisce from time to time."

Billy cuts in, "I wouldn't call every week reminiscing."

The mayor peeks over toward a table and whispers, "Between us, the city council is close to giving it away to a developer. I'm not happy about it, but my hands are tied."

"And do what with it?" Nutsy asks.

Squalo and Leo roam in through the front entrance. Leo has one crutch so he's gimping along. Squalo catches eyes with Nutsy and whispers, "He's already up the mayor's ass."

"Fuck him and his ass kissing father-in-law too," Leo whispers back.

The mayor has been anxious to develop the abandoned complex into something special and replies, "I don't have a choice anymore, Nuccio. It's been sitting vacant for years now."

Billy cuts in, "I knew it would eventually give way to a residential project. That's where the money is today."

"Who's the developer?" Nutsy asks.

"Miguel."

Billy asks, "Miguel from the Bronx?"

The mayor nods yes and replies, "I would love to keep it as a sports park but no developers believe it could be profitable. This city just can't afford to back anymore losing propositions."

Billy replies, "Are they getting special financing from the urban and planning board?"

"If I told you, you'd probably get sick about the deal that's on the table right now," the mayor replies.

Nutsy turns away. He never wanted that property to become anything but a sports park.

Billy asks, "Why give it to a Bronx guy? We have Papo right in our own backyard."

"He was my first pick, but apparently they feel he has too many projects going on right now. If he goes bust, a lot of progress goes down the drain."

While the mayor shakes hands and kisses another guest hello, she turns back toward Nutsy and says, "You figure out a way for it to be profitable, and I'll get you in front of the board. You better hurry though."

The mayor hugs another guest and Billy whispers into Nutsy's ear, "Fucking Miguel? He was the one backing Leo years ago."

As Squalo and Leo wander through the room, heads turn toward Leo wondering how he made it out of jail so early. Some of the guests are business owners that Leo used to shakedown, so they are not currently happy seeing him around again.

"Oh, great, the hag's here too," Squalo says to Leo as Kathy, N-J, and Carmela walk in.

So Leo turns and watches them walk toward a table in the front of the room and mumbles, "Yeah, sure, go right to the front table."

Squalo catches eyes with Papo and Paulie. They are usually not present at any fundraisers but have decided to come since Leo got out. They want to see how Leo acts first hand and if they can figure out what his intentions are going forward.

Papo already controls the majority of development in the city, so he usually buys a few tables and lets his subcontractors enjoy the day. This year is different though, because of the rumors he's hearing.

Paulie still has his own concerns. Over the years, he convinced the head of his family to invest in his brother's properties. He guaranteed them his brother has the city locked up with no competition. Knowing Nutsy is around has also helped throughout the years since Nutsy was never interested in city developing and always tried to keep the streets somewhat clean.

Nutsy was approached by the head of Paulie's family years back, but Paulie convinced his boss to let Nutsy operate on his own because the big money is in developing and not sports booking. Since Paulie is Papo's brother, he knows very well what transpired years ago between Papo and Nutsy and always assumed Nutsy would be on board if another situation needed to be corrected within this city.

A few minutes later, Belo wanders in and then Donnola follows after finishing his conversation with the federal agent. Donnola seems on edge like he usually does.

The room has approximately thirty tables of ten seats each. It's a spectacular room with hanging crystal chandeliers and a view of the Long Island Sound from the back terrace. The cream colored wallpaper illuminates from the glare of the sun since it's a fabulous fall day. Most plates have been sold for two hundred dollars each making it another successful turnout.

Nutsy walks up behind Papo and Paulie at the bar and sarcastically says, "Now I know it's a party when the Zetti brothers show up."

Nutsy exchanges a handshake with both of them as Paulie replies, "Now I know why I always hated these things."

Nutsy laughs and replies, "Ah… ya get used to them after a while. It's good to show your face."

Papo asks, "How's Lawrence?"

"He's bustin' balls again, so I would say okay."

Paulie says, "Yeah, Papo told me what happened. Any word yet?"

"Nothing, we got ears out though. Ya know this city can't keep a secret for too long."

"Do these two shitheads have anything to do with it?" Papo nods toward Squalo and Leo.

"We'll find out soon… let me ask ya something. Did ya bid on the sports park?"

"Yeah, years ago, but they shot it down. They said I'd have too many residential units in production."

"Apparently, Miguel has a good shot at it."

"Nah, never happen. He's an outsider."

"I just heard it from the horse's mouth," Nutsy replies.

Paulie cuts in, "I'll tell you now, if any outsiders are coming in, it's my family not that slime ball."

CHAPTER 8

Squalo, Leo, Belo, and Donnola are now sitting at a table together during the fundraiser with Miguel and his associates. Miguel operates a large construction firm and scrap metal yard in the Bronx. Leo knows him very well from the past since Miguel helped him dispose of stolen cars after Leo had stripped them for his business.

Leo would bill the insurance company for parts on new jobs but use the stolen parts and pocket the money. He would of course, throw Miguel money for getting rid of the evidence, so they have already been partners in crime.

Miguel didn't mind since he was making money on both ends, from Leo's pay off and scrapping the metal on the back end.

Papo and Leo catch eyes from across the room. Leo decides to limp over to say hello since he wants Papo to know he's planning on sticking around and making his presence known. Leo offers his hand to Papo and says, "Been a long time, Papo. I understand they call you The Pope now."

So Papo laughs if off and replies, "Yeah, I guess. You know everyone's got a nickname in this town."

"You came a long way from running numbers, ha?"

"Yeah, another life ago."

"Listen, a good friend of mine runs an electrical business and I would appreciate you giving him some work."

"I have my guys already that have been with me for years."

"So who do you kick up to?"

"No one."

"No one? The Pope gets a pass?"

"There's never any passes around here, you know that. Besides, it doesn't concern you anyway."

Paulie walks up behind Leo and blurts out, "Is there a problem here?" Paulie despises Leo and wants him to know that. Papo on the other hand, is a bit more diplomatic and he has his reasons to be.

"I guess there seems to be now," Leo sarcastically replies.

"You better keep your nose out of where it doesn't belong," Paulie doesn't hold back and throws out a threat.

Leo replies with a stern tone, "My nose belongs where I say it belongs."

Paulie gets in Leo's face but Papo quickly steps in between to separate them. "Let's end this conversation here," Papo says.

Leo glares at Paulie as he limps away. Paulie turns toward Papo and asks, "What are you butting in for?"

"This isn't the place."

Leo sits back down at his table and mumbles, "I'll stick my fucking nose anywhere I want to, you pretty boy fake gangster."

Squalo peeks over toward Leo and asks, "What are you talking about?"

"Nothing that concerns you."

Nutsy takes a seat at the head table with his family as Blackie enters the room. Leo notices her and mutters, "Oh great. This bitch is here now?"

Blackie exchanges hugs and kisses with everyone at Nutsy's table and takes a seat. Nutsy can see the agitated look on her face. She couldn't give two shits about being here. She just wants to confront Leo and Squalo.

N-J slides one of the knives on the table toward himself. Kathy quickly grabs it and asks, "What did we say before?"

"I just wanted to see it. It looks different."

"Never mind. Keep your hands off of them."

Nutsy catches eyes with Blackie and says, "Take a walk outside with me for a minute." Nutsy stands up and waits for Blackie. She hesitantly stands up and leads Nutsy outside on the terrace.

"I'm not in the mood for a lecture today, just so you know," Blackie starts off the conversation.

"Listen, things are gonna work out as they're supposed to. Trust me."

"Oh yeah, when?"

"Blackie, this ain't the old days. Everything needs to be carefully thought out –"

"No problem. While you're carefully trying to figure it out, I'll take care of it." Blackie moves toward the door without waiting for a response.

Blackie takes a seat at the table. Nutsy follows behind and takes his seat. Kathy peeks toward Blackie, then Nutsy. She can tell their conversation did not go well by the look on their faces.

Sammy and Bono enter the room and head toward the front table.

Squalo notices Sammy and mutters, "Oh, this one now too?"

Belo takes a glimpse and notices Bono heading toward Nutsy's table with Sammy. "I'll be right back," Belo says as he stands up and moves in Bono's direction.

Belo approaches Nutsy's table and says hello to everyone. "I need to speak with you," Belo says to Bono.

Bono heads out of the room with Belo, and Nutsy says to Sammy, "Out of all the friends ya could've picked, ya pick this guy's nephew?"

"Why, you always got along with Belo."

While Belo and Bono stand in the hallway, Belo blurts out, "What are you coming to all my affairs now?"

"What did I do?"

"You knew I was coming here."

"She asked me to come. What am I supposed to say?" Bono did know his uncle was coming, but he wanted to spend more time with Sammy.

So Belo hesitates and then asks, "You like this girl, or what?"

Bono doesn't reply and Belo becomes impatient. "I asked you a question."

"I do… I like her a lot." Bono finally commits to his true feelings.

"What are we talking about here? As a friend or –"

"More than a friend."

"I thought you were –"

"I was, but for some reason I'm attracted to her." Bono wants to be certain his uncle knows he cares deeply for Sammy.

Belo stares for a moment then hesitantly replies, "Behave… I have enough problems right now and don't need you creating anymore, understand?"

Bono nods in agreement.

Nutsy's cell phone rings while sitting at his table and he answers, "Yeah."

Binky, the Bronx bookie, is sitting at a table in his restaurant on Arthur Avenue. "Do I smell or something?" Binky sarcastically asks.

"Hey, Binky, what's up?"

"You haven't visited my new restaurant yet."

"I'll get there, I promise. There's just a lot of shit going on now."

"I heard that creep's son got out," Binky says.

"Yup, I'm staring at his ugly mug as we speak."

"Where?"

"Would ya believe this prick showed up to the city fundraiser with his father?"

"I'm not surprised at all. Let me ask you, is Miguel there too?"

Nutsy peeks over toward Leo's table. "Yup."

"I heard Miguel already has the drawings made up. Two-hundred and fifty units with retail stores. A goldmine if it hits, like hitting the lotto."

"For what?"

"That shithole on the east side of your city that's been vacant for years."

"How do ya know?"

"Hey, your city ain't the only close-knit one that talks in New York... and another thing you gotta know, the weasel's chirping."

"To who?"

"A Fed."

"Ya positive?"

"I saw it with my own eyes, the same prick that was busting my balls years back."

"We gotta talk. I'll call ya later." Nutsy hangs up and takes a glimpse toward Squalo's table. They're all laughing it up and seem to be having a great time.

Leo says to Miguel, "I'll mortgage the shop and put up a large chunk. I wanna be an investor in your project and stick it up his ass."

"What's with you and Nutsy? He's always been respectful to me."

"That prick put us out –"

Squalo cuts in, "Listen, we're here to have a good time and to see how this game works out."

Leo replies, "Fuck the game. We got new shit on the horizon." Leo is feeling good. The few rum and cokes he drank have already hit him.

Staci moves toward the front of the room and takes the podium. "Good afternoon and welcome. It's wonderful to see so many familiar faces. We would like to thank everyone for their continued support. This administration wouldn't be where it is without each and every one of you. I even noticed a few people in the room who haven't been here in years, so it's an exciting day for our city."

Leo whispers into Squalo's ear, "Is this that daughter of the old mayor?"

Squalo nods yes.

Nutsy glances toward Sammy and Bono who happen to be oblivious to what's going on. They're staring at one another with sparks in their eyes. Kathy peeks toward Nutsy and he nods toward Sammy for Kathy to take a glimpse. She glances over and shrugs her shoulders at Nutsy. All Nutsy can think about is, of anyone she can pick, he's gotta be Belo's nephew? Although he feels Bono is respectful and not a threat to his daughter, it's the fact that he's Belo's nephew that bothers him.

Staci introduces Billy to say a few words and Billy stands up as the crowd cheers him on. He is surely a respected city party member.

Squalo mutters, "Fuck you and your fake white teeth."

Leo peers around with an annoyed look since he can tell the guests love Billy by their reactions while Billy now stands next to Staci.

N-J whispers to Nutsy, "Dad, I have to go to the bathroom."

Nutsy whispers back, "Okay, it's right outside the door."

While N-J heads toward a door, Donnola excuses himself at his table and sneaks out a door in the back of the room. Donnola makes his way into the bathroom and stands next to N-J by a urinal. "Hey, your, N-J, right?"

"Yes, do I know you?"

"I'm an old neighbor of yours. I haven't seen you since you were a young boy. You got so big and handsome."

N-J just nods and pulls up his zipper. "Do you gamble at all like your father does?" Donnola asks.

"No, he won't let me."

"How about we make a bet? There's a raft out in the water. I'll bet you a thousand dollars you can't make it there and back." Donnola already knows N-J can't swim.

"A thousand dollars? That's a lot of money, but I can't swim."

"I'll make it even sweeter for you to try. How about five thousand?"

"Five thousand?" N-J's eyes open wide.

"Yeah, let's see what you got."

N-J hesitantly replies, "I'll think about it."

Donnola opens the door and replies, "This is between you and me. A REAL man's bet." He walks out.

N-J sits back down at the table while Billy addresses the crowd. After Billy introduces the mayor, he takes a seat at Nutsy's table.

While the mayor thanks everyone for their support and contributions, N-J catches eyes with Donnola who gives him a nod toward the water. He attempts to edge N-J on.

Sammy would like to take a stroll around the grounds with Bono, so she excuses herself. "We're gonna take a walk for a minute."

Nutsy replies, "Now? We're eating soon."

"We'll eat when we get back." Sammy glances toward Bono and says, "Come on. I need some air."

Bono stays still since he's concerned about Nutsy and doesn't want to appear disrespectful. Nutsy reluctantly gives him a nod to go, so Bono stands up and follows Sammy out of the room.

Nutsy whispers to Kathy, "Why is it always something with her?"

"She's a teenager, that's why."

CHAPTER 9

Sammy and Bono step outside and take in the grounds. The spectacular view of the Long Island Sound is mesmerizing as they both gaze toward the never ending body of water. The glimmer off small rippling waves makes the scene even more romantic. Mature colored oak and maple trees sway in the light breeze, which are surrounded by borders of orange, yellow, and red colored mums.

N-J catches eyes with Donnola who nods toward the water to edge N-J on again. After a minute, N-J excuses himself to go to the bathroom since he's finally ready for the challenge. Nutsy asks, "Didn't ya just go?"

"I have to go again."

Kathy replies, "Leave your sister alone." Kathy feels N-J wants to follow his sister around like he usually does.

N-J leaves the room and then makes a move toward the beach area. He peeks back to see if anyone is watching and quickly removes his jacket and kicks off his shoes. He takes in a deep breath and then dives into the water. Since he's not a swimmer, N-J attempts to doggie paddle toward the raft which is about a hundred feet out.

The romantic view has gotten to Sammy and Bono as they are now lip to lip in their own world. Bono is a good kisser and Sammy can't get enough of him.

N-J's quickly losing steam since his soaked pants are weighing him down. He pauses to catch his breath but dips under. His head pops back up for a second and he screams, "Help! Help!" N-J's in trouble and he senses it.

Bono pauses for a second while kissing Sammy since he thinks he recognizes N-J's voice in the distance and curiously glances toward the water.

"Help!" N-J's head dips back under the water.

"Holy shit! I think that's your brother out there."

"Where?"

"In the water."

"The water! He can't swim!" Sammy and Bono frantically bolt toward the water when Sammy's heel gets caught between two wood planks and she yells, "Ah!" She falls onto the wood deck since her ankle twisted after her heel had gotten stuck. She attempts to stand up but falls back down. "Go help him. Please!"

Bono nervously races toward the water. N-J's head bobs in and out of the water while nervously paddling his hands. His body is now cold and tired. He's losing his breath and becoming extremely anxious.

Sammy frantically presses a button on her cell phone while hopping toward the water in extreme pain. Nutsy peeks at his phone as it buzzes and curiously answers, "Is everything all right?"

"Dad! N-J's in the water! I think he's drowning!"

"What!" Nutsy leaps up and bolts toward the side door.

Bono finally reaches N-J's location, but N-J's head dips under the water again. N-J doesn't have any more energy and is completely exhausted. So Bono dives down searching for N-J in the dark water and feels around in different directions hoping to latch onto him.

Although Sammy's in tears and can't believe this is happening, her adrenaline is enough for her to put pressure on her injured ankle and finally make it to the water.

Nutsy, Kathy, Blackie, and Carmela finally make it to the water. Some guests nervously pile onto the terrace to witness what is happening.

Bono has finally grabbed hold of N-J under the water and pulls him up toward the surface. He attempts to tow N-J back to shore, but it's a real struggle. His wet clothes are also weighing him down and he's totally exhausted. Nutsy chucks off his jacket and dives into the water and nervously strokes toward N-J and Bono.

Belo stands on the terrace with the other guys trying to figure out what is happening. He notices Bono's head in the water and darts across the beach while the other three stand and just watch. They are not interested in helping at all.

Nutsy finally reaches Bono and grabs hold of N-J's arm. They both tow him back to shore attempting to keep N-J's head above water. Nutsy can tell that Bono is losing steam and asks, "Are you okay?"

Bono nods yes and continues to help. Although he's worn out, Bono's determined to help get N-J back to safety. Nutsy feels a twinge in his chest, but he continues tugging N-J towards the shore. All he can think about is let me get my son to shore and then take me.

They finally make it to the shoreline and hover over N-J who is now lying on his back not breathing and Nutsy frantically yells out, "Does anyone know C-P-R?!"

Belo squats down and gets to work. Belo used to be a lifeguard at a local pool named Wilson when he was a teenager and learning C-P-R was a requirement. Kathy's in tears while watching and Blackie wraps her arms around her to console her. Carmela is in shock and makes the sign of the cross. At this point, it appears bleak at best.

A crowd nervously gathers around to watch the outcome. Belo is pumping hard and giving N-J mouth to mouth but he hasn't responded yet.

Donnola watches with Squalo and Leo on the terrace. They couldn't give a shit and it shows by their half-assed reactions.

N-J's head finally lunges forward and a burst of water ejects from his mouth. Kathy and Sammy embrace N-J who is now breathing heavily but at least conscious. Blackie hugs Carmela who makes another sign of the cross.

Belo sighs and closes his eyes. Although he has issues with Nutsy, the last thing he would want to see is something happening to one of his children. He moves in Bono's direction to check on him.

Nutsy yells out, "Belo!" So Belo turns and Nutsy sincerely says, "Thank you."

Belo nods and continues to head toward Bono who appears to be fine while hugging Sammy.

Donnola peeks at his watch and says, "I gotta run. Something came up."

Nutsy glances toward the terrace and notices Donnola, Squalo, and Leo standing by the rail. If this was one of their sons, regardless of their business situation, Nutsy would never take this as lightly as they have. His insides are burning up with fire. He has tried to remain calm and let things roll off his shoulder, but if he doesn't like the answer he gets when he finally questions N-J, all bets are off.

Squalo says, "What the fuck are they all making a fuss about, his son's fine."

"I'll call you later." Donnola is in a rush to leave since N-J could eye witness him.

"Where you going? The game hasn't even started yet," Squalo asks.

"Something important came up." Donnola darts back inside.

Leo asks Squalo, "What could be more important than the game?"

Squalo replies, "Who the fuck knows with this guy."

N-J is finally able to stand up and Kathy holds him tightly. She can't believe what has happened. Nutsy is dying to question N-J since he's a skeptic and believes there's an underlying reason N-J was in the water knowing very well he can't swim.

As Belo approaches Squalo and Leo on the terrace, Squalo asks, "What the fuck did you help him for?"

"How could you even ask me that?"

The guests are all relieved that N-J appears to be okay and start drifting back inside.

Billy was in the bathroom at the time this had all happened and has now made it to the water. "What the hell's going on?"

Kathy replies, "Not now, dad, we'll talk later."

Billy glances toward Nutsy who is now soaking wet. He has seen this irate look on Nutsy's face from the past and knows whatever happened can't be a good thing. So Nutsy says to Billy, "We're gonna go."

Billy doesn't want to get into it with Nutsy and knows he's twisted inside so he just nods in agreement. Plus, Nutsy's clothes are dripping wet.

Nutsy says to Kathy, "Let's go." Nutsy's wet hair drips on his face and shirt as he heads toward the parking lot.

"Dad, I can't walk. I twisted my ankle."

Bono is extremely worn out but says, "Here, I'll give you a piggy back." He turns so Sammy could hop on his back.

Sammy doesn't wait for Nutsy's response and hops up on Bono's back with one foot.

"I'm out of here too," Blackie says.

As they all head toward the parking lot, Nutsy loses his patience and asks N-J, "What the hell were ya doin' in the water alone?"

Kathy says, "Not now. Leave it alone."

"Fuck that!" Nutsy is fired up. He can't help himself and grabs N-J's arm and stops him short. "I asked ya a fuckin' question."

N-J breaks down into tears. He knows his father is livid, but N-J is also embarrassed to say the truth.

"Stop it now!" Kathy yells out.

The last thing Nutsy would ever want to do is upset his son, but this is different. He suspects there is more to this and needs to know. "Look at me," Nutsy says to N-J.

N-J hesitantly peeks toward Nutsy, but looks back down. "I'm not mad at you. I just wanna know why ya did this, and you're gonna tell me."

Kathy starts to interject and Nutsy cuts her off, "This is between me and N-J now."

Kathy sighs since she knows Nutsy will not leave this alone until he gets his answer. N-J looks at Kathy for her approval. So Kathy hesitantly says, "It's alright. We're both not mad at you. Tell your father."

N-J hesitantly replies, "I made a bet with our old neighbor I can swim to the raft and back."

"What old neighbor?" Kathy asks.

"I don't know his name or remember him."

"What does he look like?" Nutsy asks.

"He's kind of short, no hair, and has a big nose."

So Nutsy says to Kathy, "Take him home. I'll meet ya at the house."

"Dad, what about my ankle?"

"Go home and ice it." Nutsy heads back toward the room.

"What are you doing?" Kathy asks.

"Just take 'em home," Nutsy replies while heading into the hall.

Kathy says to Billy, "Please, make sure he doesn't do anything stupid."

Nutsy approaches Squalo and Leo's table. Miguel is feeling pretty good right about now and sarcastically blurts out, "The King of the four-square miles."

Nutsy totally ignores his comment and asks, "Where's Donnola?" Nutsy feels it was Donnola by N-J's description.

Leo sarcastically replies, "Go check the cheese store." They all bust out in laughter since they've already had plenty of drinks.

So Nutsy and Leo catch eyes. Leo can sense Nutsy's twisted inside and stands up to provoke him further. Squalo hops up and stands in between them and says, "He said something important came up and had to leave."

"Yeah, that's convenient."

"I'm not his keeper," Squalo replies.

The mayor takes the podium and says, "Thank God everything turned out okay. We'll be starting again soon. Please take your seats."

Billy approaches Squalo's table and says to Nutsy, "Go home and get changed."

Nutsy still has his eyes fixated on Leo. He's burning up inside but knows it's not the place or time.

So Leo sarcastically says to Miguel, "I told you he got softer. Imagine if this was the old days?"

Nutsy makes a quick move toward Leo, but Billy grabs hold of his arm and says, "Leave, now!"

Billy knows very well Nutsy is twisted up inside and doesn't want him to do anything he'll regret tomorrow. "Go, I said!" Billy insists.

Nutsy storms away and out of the room.

Leo says, "Fucking guy doesn't even have any respect."

"Enjoy the rest of the party," Billy replies and heads back toward his table.

Kathy, N-J, and Carmela drive back toward their house. Sammy decided to ride back with Bono since they came together. Everyone is quiet in Kathy's car while N-J stares out the window of the back seat. He knows he made a bad decision and that his parents are mad at him. The worst part is, he's embarrassed that everyone witnessed he couldn't swim.

Although Sammy's ankle is throbbing and has swelled up, she can't help but stare at Bono. Besides saving her brother, she thinks what he achieved today was a remarkable act of bravery and a true turn on. His wet hair is now slicked back, and her eyes are glued on his chiseled cheek bones.

Nutsy flies down the road in his car when his Bluetooth rings and he answers, "I don't wanna get into it."

Billy is on the other end and says, "Don't do anything you'll regret. Go straight home."

"I'll call ya back." Nutsy hangs up from Billy and presses Binky's number.

Binky answers while sitting at the bar in his restaurant, "The fundraiser's –"

"We gotta talk."

"What happened?" Binky can tell Nutsy's aggravated.

"I'll meet ya outside at the clam bar."

CHAPTER 10

Kathy pulls up in front of her house and notices Nutsy's car isn't around. She gets an uncomfortable feeling since she knows Nutsy's livid and not home as of yet.

They all walk inside the house and Kathy calls Nutsy's cell phone. He notices her name displaying on the dashboard of his car but doesn't answer. So Kathy dials again and it's the same routine, Nutsy purposely ignores her call. Kathy hangs up and dials Blackie, who is now in her foyer and asks, "Did you hear from Nutsy?"

"Nope."

"I called him twice and he's not answering."

"Yeah, probably on purpose. I'll try him."

So, Blackie dials Nutsy and he ignores her call also. He has no interest in discussing anything at this moment. He knows N-J is okay and that he's safe with Kathy now.

He'll allow certain things to slide, but not this. Trying to make a business move is one thing, but a rat is totally unacceptable in his book and he also suspects it was Donnola who N-J was describing to him.

Billy's still at the catering hall waiting for the fundraiser to end. He's usually the life of the party but has no interest in being here at this time. He dials Kathy's phone and asks, "Is he there?"

"No."

"Shit! Alright, let me run." Billy hangs up and dials Nutsy's number. Nutsy's Bluetooth rings in his car and he ignores Billy's call also, so Billy hangs up with an annoyed look.

Nutsy finally meets up with Binky at the clam bar on the border of the Bronx and New Row. Binky is about sixty-years-old and has known Nutsy for a long time. They have always respected each other and never went against one another. Binky is well aware of what transpired years ago with The Westerns since they were from downtown and always thanked Nutsy in a way. The Westerns had Binky's area locked up also at that time, so he always felt Nutsy saved his business, and possibly his life.

Nutsy has always felt if he ever decided to walk away from the rackets, Binky would be a perfect person to offer his operation to. Nutsy and Binky are both similar in style and demeanor, but Binky is considered an outsider since he's not part of Westchester County and may not be welcomed by the community. At this point, Nutsy doesn't seem to care anymore.

After they agreed on certain topics of interest to both of them, Binky asks, "Why me, Nutsy? Why do I get this opportunity?"

"Hey, I'll offer it to someone else if ya want."

Binky laughs and replies, "I always enjoyed your sense of humor, but you'll be screwing Ladro this way."

"No I won't. I'll be doing him a favor, trust me."

"That's what you say… I don't wanna take on any other headaches. I got enough in my life already."

"Ya let me deal with Ladro, alright?"

Binky nods and hesitantly replies, "I gotta say, Billy has taught you well."

"I'm just tryin' to be around for my family as long as I can." Nutsy latches onto his chest.

"What's wrong?"

"Ah, nothing… just a little gas here and there… can I count on you?"

"I'll tell you what, Nutsy. I'm gonna take care of the first thing just to show you I'm on board. He's gotta go anyway and you're too close to the vest."

The same lady is walking her dog again in the woods by where Vito's body lies under a pile of leaves and brush. Her dog is barking relentlessly again in the same place as earlier, roughly about ten feet away. She now becomes suspicious and allows her dog to guide her to what is troubling it.

Her dog stops right near the pile of leaves and continues barking away, this time uncontrollably. Her dog begins to dig at the pile of leaves and Vito's leg becomes exposed. The lady begins to scream at the top of her lungs.

After finishing his meeting with Binky, Nutsy decides to take a quick ride passed Donnola's apartment in New Row. Not that he doesn't trust Binky, but Nutsy's the type of person who likes to see things first-hand. Maybe it's a form of paranoia, but it's the only way for Nutsy to feel one hundred percent certain.

He doesn't notice Donnola's car parked outside so he circles around a few blocks. He finally spots Donnola's car parked and notices what appears to be a marked car idling across the street with a person sitting in the driver's and passenger seat.

Nutsy quickly pulls over behind another car approximately fifty feet away and watches.

The lady now stands in shock with a few police officers by Vito's body. Red lights twirl in the street and a few bystanders curiously pause by the marked off area. It's been very quiet in this part of the city and has some residents now on edge.

The passenger door of the marked car opens and Donnola steps out and makes a quick move toward his car across the street.

Nutsy notices Donnola and mumbles, "Ya fuckin' rodent."

The marked car takes off and Donnola's car follows. Nutsy waits a second and then pulls out.

Ladro is having a heated discussion with a nurse in his hospital room. He wants to leave but she's insisting he has to stay as per doctor's orders. He wants no part of it, so the nurse looks at a clipboard and says, "I'm calling your wife."

"She's at a party. Call my friend Nuccio, he's second on the list." Ladro figures Nutsy would be on his side before Blackie would.

So the nurse dials Nutsy's number and waits. Nutsy still circles the block following Donnola who is trying to find a space, but can't. Nutsy's Bluetooth rings and he answers, "Yeah."

The nurse asks, "Is this Mr. Gento?"

"Yeah, who's asking?"

"Hi, sir, I'm calling from the hospital and I think you need to get here as soon as possible."

Nutsy becomes a little nervous and asks, "Don't tell me he flatlined again?"

"No, it's quite the opposite. He's making a scene and is trying to leave. I can't control him anymore."

Ladro yells out in the background, "Get me the hell atta here, Nutsy!"

"See, sir."

"Put him on."

The nurse hands the phone to Ladro and he says, "The guy in the next bed snores like a fucking rhinoceros. You either pick me up or I'm walking out."

Nutsy sighs and replies, "I'll be right there. Don't leave."

"If you ain't here in fifteen minutes, I'll meet you at the bar." Ladro hangs up the call.

"This fuckin' guy." Nutsy hangs up the call.

Two police officers enter Belinda's office and she immediately gets nervous since she suspects something is not right. "Are you the owner?" one of the officers asks.

"Well, kinda. Is there a problem?"

"We found one of your workers dead in the woods on the north side of town."

"What?! Who?" Belinda's eyes open wide.

The officer hands off one of Vito's business cards to Belinda and her eyes close. She immediately suspects her brother might have something to do with this. "It looks like he was one of your workers," the officer says.

Belinda tries to remain calm and asks, "Yes he is, what happened?"

"We aren't positive yet, but he was badly beaten and apparently dumped."

"No wonder he never answered. I was calling him all day."

"Do you know of anyone who could've done this to him?"

"Not off the top of my head, the guys all get along here."

"Okay." The officer hands off a card to Belinda and says, "I'm gonna need to speak to all the workers."

Belinda nods in agreement. She suspects this is Leo's doing.

Nutsy heads toward the hospital to deal with Ladro's issue. He dials Binky's number and Binky answers while strolling down Arthur Avenue, "You see him?"

"Yeah, you were right."

"Listen, I know you have issues with Belo, but I'm taking him along for the ride with me."

"No fuckin' way."

"Look, we all make mistakes in life. He never thought you'd take it this far... at least hear him out when you come down."

"I know he's your brother-in-law, but that ain't my problem."

"All our problems somehow become all of our problems... do me this favor and hear him out."

Nutsy's not crazy about this but thinks he at least owes Belo the benefit of the doubt for saving his son's life.

The football game is starting in ten minutes. This is the game of the year. 'The fix' as most people call it, a game where gamblers could possibly break even on their yearly losses or turn their gains into a banner year. A fix only comes around so often and it hasn't surfaced for a while, so a lot of money is riding one way, on the under bet.

Bookies caught the wrong way without being able to spread out their bets could get destroyed. At this point, Nutsy isn't too concerned because of his deal with Munchie. In fact, Munchie already gave him the easy way out.

Nutsy enters Ladro's hospital room where he is currently getting dressed. "Ya can't go yet," Nutsy says.

"This place is driving me nuts. I got a rhinoceros on one side, a moaner on the other like she's getting laid all night, and the doctor's a fucking weirdo."

"Still, ya not ready. Look at you, the bandage ain't even off yet."

The nurse enters the room and asks, "See what I'm saying?"

"I got things to do, nurse. And it ain't –"

"But you're not signed out."

"Doctor Mark did." Ladro glances toward Nutsy and nods toward the door for them to leave.

The nurse takes a glimpse at a clipboard and replies, "I don't see his name on here."

"He told me personally. Let's go, Nutsy."

The nurse scurries behind Ladro and says, "Sir, Mr. Tisi, you can't leave like this. Your cut hasn't healed yet."

Ladro continues moving away and replies, "I'll pour whiskey on it."

The nurse pauses with an annoyed look, turns toward Nutsy and asks, "Can you please talk to him?"

"He'll listen to you before me, for sure."

The nurse stands with her hands on her hips, shakes her head, and heads back toward the nurses' station.

Nutsy and Ladro stand on the sidewalk outside of the hospital and Ladro takes in a deep breath. "I can't take the smell in there anymore. I think everyone shits their pants."

"This is crazy, ya know."

"Why, you'd stay and listen to people moan all night? Fuck that. Let's get a drink and watch the game. That's more important anyway."

CHAPTER 11

After getting into Nutsy's car and driving down the main avenue, Nutsy and Ladro pull up in front of Sista. They both enter Sista and take a seat on stools by the bar. While the barmaid approaches them from behind the bar, Nutsy notices a distraught look on her face and asks, "Is everything all right?"

She hesitantly replies, "I know you won't care, but I think Vito's missing."

"What do you mean missing?" Ladro questions her since he has every intention of searching for him at a later time.

"I don't know. He's not returning my calls, and no one has heard from him."

So Nutsy and Ladro catch eyes. They are different in nature but have similar thoughts about things, and this is no different.

She places two shot glasses on the counter and fills them with scotch. She moves away toward the next customer.

Nutsy and Ladro catch eyes again like they can read each other's mind. "And so it begins," Nutsy says and then shoots it back.

"Before we put the game on, check this site out that I found while in the hospital." Ladro holds his phone out for Nutsy to see. On the screen is a lady holding a whiskey glass up in salute.

Nutsy takes a glimpse and asks, "What is that, a dating site or something?"

"Nah, far from it. It's a page where people toast and wish each other well in life. Here, I'll show you. Lift up your glass." Ladro holds his phone up to take a selfie of him and Nutsy.

"What are ya doing?" Nutsy asks.

"Come on, lift it up and smile!"

Nutsy hesitantly lifts up his glass with a half-ass smile and Ladro snaps a picture. "Jesus Christ. You could at least give a nicer smile. Let's do another one." Ladro holds up the phone for another selfie.

So Nutsy rolls his eyes while Ladro says, "Come on... and smile this time. The ladies will love us."

Nutsy hesitantly raises his glass again with a nicer smile and Ladro snaps another picture of the two of them holding up their glasses in cheer. "Alright, this is better. Watch this." Ladro posts the picture on the site and wishes everyone well from Sista Bar and Grill.

"I really think this fall made ya a little nutty," Nutsy says.

"Nah, look... four likes and two red hearts already... oh shit, ten likes and five hearts." Ladro gets excited.

"What are hearts?"

"What are hearts? That means they love us."

"This fall really did fuck ya up, didn't it?"

Ladro laughs and replies, "Nah, we gotta get you up to speed here with this stuff."

Nutsy presses the remote and raises the volume on the TV. "No thanks, I gotta nuff stuff."

Blackie enters Ladro's room and sees an empty bed. She moves toward the nurses' station and asks, "Was my husband moved to a different room?"

"Is your husband Lawrence Tisi?"

Blackie nods yes.

The nurse says, "He walked out."

"What, he just left on his own?"

"Yes… he wouldn't listen to anyone."

Blackie sighs and replies, "I know that very well. Thank you." Blackie heads toward the elevators.

Nutsy and Ladro are intently watching the game when Blackie storms in and says, "You have some nerve leaving and not even calling me."

"I was just about to."

Blackie asks Nutsy, "You let him do this? He still has the bandage on his head."

"Ya know your husband."

"You know something, fuck the both of you." Blackie glances back toward Nutsy and says, "Instead of sitting here, you should be home checking on your son and daughter." Blackie storms out.

"What's she talking about?" Ladro asks.

"I had an issue at the club. I'll tell ya later."

About ten minutes later, Billy approaches them at the bar and says to Nutsy, "Take a walk with me."

"Now? The game's on."

"I don't give a shit about the game. Let's go!" Billy moves away toward the front door.

Ladro says, "Shit, he looks pissed about something."

"I'll be right back. Don't go anywhere." Nutsy walks away.

Nutsy and Billy stroll down the busy avenue. Billy has had enough of waiting to hear about Nutsy's dream, so he says, "You're gonna tell me what it is, and now."

"Tell ya what?"

"I wanna hear what this dream's about." Billy knows things are starting to heat up and he wants Nutsy to take a different path in life.

Nutsy thinks about what Ladro had said to him in the hospital and hesitantly replies, "I need to do right by my son."

"What are you talking about? And I don't wanna hear that you can't tell me. I'm tired of listening to that bullshit."

Nutsy knows he's been keeping his thoughts to himself for a while now and hesitantly replies, "I want the sports complex to be about special needs kids. A place they can have fun and enjoy the game of baseball."

Billy sighs and says, "Nuccio, I gotta be honest. It's a beautiful gesture, but I can't see that working. What about condos or –"

Since Nutsy has finally explained what it is, he becomes agitated by Billy's comment and says, "You've been bustin' my balls for years to chase it and –"

"First off, I'm your father-in-law and I don't appreciate your tone. Secondly, you heard the mayor. There's no money in sports parks and they can't afford to fund a losing proposition."

"I heard people are paying big money to play. We just haven't been exposed to the concept in this city."

"Look, I'm not gonna lie. You know I would help you with anything. But this? Come on, Nuccio, let's be for real here."

"Ya know something. I thought of all the people, you'd be the one to have my back. I guess I was wrong."

"Alright, so tell me. Why this?"

Nutsy remains silent since his intentions are for personal reasons of his own that no one knows of, not even Kathy.

Billy stops short and yanks on Nutsy's arm, "You tell me what this is about God dammit!" Billy has had enough.

Nutsy hesitantly replies, "I want N-J to be taken care of for the rest of his life. I want this park to pay for his home in the future."

Billy has a feeling there's more to it than just this and asks, "And what else?"

"That's it." Nutsy admitted to enough already and doesn't want Billy to know more than he needs to at this time.

"Nuccio, no one today is gonna invest into your personal wishes. No profit, no investors. It's that simple."

"I know, why do ya think I haven't chased it yet? The problem is, me and Kathy ain't gonna be around forever. What happens to him then?"

"I don't know. Maybe, the state gets involved."

"Screw that! This state will never get a hold of my son. These fuckin' politicians can't even run it no less have my son's best interest in hand."

"I don't know what to say. Unless, Sammy takes –"

"I can't put this on my daughter. I want her to have her own life... I got one more idea and then I'll know for sure one way or another."

"You better hurry because that condo complex is close to taking off."

"Can you stop it?"

"Maybe, if you give me something to work with."

"I'll know after this week. Now let me watch this game."

Billy watches Nutsy head back into the bar and shakes his head. Down deep inside, Billy feels this dream of Nutsy's is a dead end.

Nutsy takes a seat next to Ladro at the bar and asks, "Did the score change?"

"Still seven nothing. The fucking Bears fumbled on the two yard line."

Nutsy looks at the TV screen and notices food on the corner of it. "How did food get up there?"

The barmaid nods toward Ladro and says, "Take a guess."

While Ladro laughs it off, Nutsy says with an annoyed look, "Will ya please stop throwin' shit at the TV? These things ain't cheap."

"Yeah, they are. You can get a seventy inch for a thousand bucks now."

"Just stop chuckin' shit, will ya please?" Nutsy takes another swig.

Ladro laughs it off.

Sammy hobbles to the couch in her living room and flops down onto it. Her ankle is blown up like a balloon. Kathy places a towel wrapped with ice on top of it. "I don't like the way this looks," Kathy says and walks away.

N-J wanders in with a nervous look on his face after eyeing Sammy on the couch. He feels horrible about what had happened to her and knows it's all because of him. "Don't tell me you're sorry again," Sammy says.

"Well, I am." N-J's eyes are fixated on the towel filled with ice.

Squalo, Leo, and Miguel stand by the bar in the catering hall. Squalo's eyes are glued to the TV. Leo couldn't give a shit about the game, just that it could hurt Nutsy badly, and he hopes it does. As far as Squalo benefiting, Leo thinks his father's already doing just fine in life.

Squalo laughs and says, "Another fumble on the five yard line. Yup the fix is on." So Squalo raises his glass up and salutes Miguel.

Miguel asks, "You got my fifty grand in, right?"

"You better believe I did."

Papo and Paulie wander over toward the bar and Paulie whispers, "I can't stand this asshole."

"Don't start anything. We're right in the middle of the project," Papo replies.

Papo and Paulie order drinks and stand on the opposite end of the bar. Miguel peeks over toward Squalo and whispers, "When you guys take back over, first thing you gotta do is knock off The Pope. I want those towers he's got going."

Leo replies, "The Pope has seen his better days, trust me. His time's ticking... and that piece of shit brother he has that thinks he's a Godfather now."

Squalo replies, "Yeah, how the hell he made capo is beyond me."

Miguel replies, "He can't be touched but Papo is fair game."

Leo replies, "Everyone's fair game as far as I'm concerned. Lions don't discriminate."

Blackie enters the body shop and into Leo's office. Belinda is currently packing up boxes with her belongings. "Are you sure they're not on the way back yet?" Blackie asks.

"My brother just called from the club to make sure my stuff is out by today."

"I still can't believe they're doing this to you... well then again, I guess I can. What did you want to talk about?"

"Can you get me a job at the bank? I'll do anything. I just wanna get the fuck away from them."

"If anything, it will be a teller's position."

"Fine." Belinda just wants out and to be able to move on with her life.

"Banks don't pay much, Belinda."

"I just want a clear head, a change in life… if I could only get back at them somehow."

"Well, you kinda can."

"How?" Belinda curiously asks.

CHAPTER 12

Nutsy swigs back the whiskey glass while glaring at the TV. The screen displays Packers 7 and Bears 10.

"This fucking game should be twenty-twenty right now. I think they put butter on that ball for this game," Ladro says.

"Two fumbles and an interception within the ten yard line and you don't think they know what they're doing?" Nutsy asks.

"Who knows, maybe the second half line in Vegas will make a difference."

"Look at us, glued to this TV like two jamokes."

"Jamokes? Shit, I haven't heard that one in years." Ladro laughs.

"Yeah, that's exactly what we are."

Nutsy's cell phone rings and he answers, "Yeah."

"Where are you?" Kathy asks from their kitchen.

"Watching the game with Ladro."

"In his room?"

"No, the bar."

"How the hell did they sign him out? He looked horrible yesterday."

"They didn't, he signed himself out."

"Whatever… I don't even wanna know. Your son's looking for you. He thinks you hate him now."

"I'll be home soon. Tell him we can watch it together."

"And your daughter's ankle doesn't look good."

"Tell her to keep the ice on. I'll see ya soon." Nutsy hangs up.

Ladro takes a sip of his drink and says, "Alright, second quarter's starting."

Ladro's cell phone rings and he answers, "What's up?"

Blackie's driving down the avenue in her car and replies, "I want you home. I don't trust your judgment right now."

"Oh, thanks for the vote of confidence."

"Just get your ass home and stop screwing around." Blackie hangs up.

"Now they're both calling," Ladro whispers to Nutsy.

"After this quarter, I'll drive ya home. I gotta spend time with N-J before he leaves."

The fundraiser is still going on but guests are now glued to the flat screen TV behind the bar. Most in the room have wagered on this game and are eager to watch the final results.

A lot has happened in the game so far and it appears the fix is in place, so Squalo is a happy man at this moment. Leo's watching but couldn't give a shit since he has no money on the line or couldn't benefit in any other ways.

Billy is home right now sitting in his wood paneled sunroom and thinking about his earlier conversation with Nutsy. Although he's been trying to get Nutsy out of the rackets, he now thinks his earlier conversation with Nutsy could hit a brick wall. Many builders have already proposed a sports complex but just couldn't figure out a way to make it profitable.

Nutsy getting out has been Billy's personal dream for years, but he just can't see Nutsy's agenda working. How does he make it profitable? Billy's somewhat discouraged since he knows the city will never buy into it regardless of his political ties. He would rather see Nutsy attempt a residential complex.

It's now halfway through the second quarter and the score's the same. After a long run back, the Bears are currently on the Pac's thirty-yard line and just threw an interception. Ladro is pissed off and hurls his French fries at the screen. "He was doubled covered you fucking asshole!"

"Will ya stop throwin' shit at the screen?" Nutsy yells out.

The barmaid picks up a napkin to wipe ketchup off the edge of the screen and Nutsy says, "Let HIM do it."

"It's alright," she replies.

"I'll do it." Ladro moves behind the bar and wipes the ketchup off the TV. "How does that look?"

"Ya missed a spot on the corner."

"Now you're gonna bust my balls?" Ladro glances at the TV. "Look… look at the replay. Two guys are on his ass. Maybe he bet the under too, this thief."

Nutsy laughs and asks, "Oh, now the quarterback's a thief?"

"Everyone's a thief in one way or another… alright, go home to your family. I'll stick around."

"I'm takin' ya home. Let's go." Nutsy stands up.

"I'm alright. I'll play around on the eight o'clock site."

So Nutsy stands there and gives Ladro a look like, I said let's go.

Ladro laughs, stands up and follows Nutsy out of the front door.

While they both head home in Nutsy's car, Ladro says, "Take a ride around the park. I wanna see if that punk's around."

"Tomorrow's another day. You're in no shape right now." They both have no idea about Vito yet.

"Was that asshole Miguel around today?"

"Yup, sitting with the stooges," Nutsy replies while spinning through the roundabout.

"That's another guy I can't stand… with his hubcap shop, his fake construction company. You know he helped Leo with the pistols, right?"

"Who doesn't?"

Nutsy pulls up in front of Ladro's house and Ladro gets out of the car. "Listen, I know we didn't discuss this, but no more of that shit. You hear me?" Nutsy says.

"What shit?"

"Don't play dumb with me."

"It was just for the job."

"Then it shouldn't be an issue since the job's completed, right?"

Ladro nods and walks away from the car.

Nutsy yells out, "I wanna hear it!"

Ladro turns and replies, "What are we in fucking kindergarten now?"

Nutsy just stares waiting for a reply.

"I'm not doing it anymore, okay?" Ladro moves toward his house and mumbles, "Now he thinks he's my father."

"I heard that!" Nutsy yells out the window of the car.

"Good, you were supposed to."

While Nutsy watches Ladro enter his house, he gets a sharp pain down his side. He always wondered if he would go early like his father did, but never got pains like this before.

Maybe it's just stress he thinks, or maybe, my life is finally catching up with me. He hits the gas and takes off toward his house.

Nutsy enters his house and Billy meets him in the foyer. Billy made a trip to Nutsy's house to finish their conversation from earlier since Billy was uncomfortable with the way it ended.

Billy says, "It's ten-seven. Third quarter just started."

"I know."

"Take a quick walk with me," Billy says.

"Now?"

"Yeah, just down the block and back."

While Nutsy and Billy stroll down the street, Billy needs to get a few things off of his chest. "Look, I know I discouraged you before –"

"I'm disappointed, Billy. I finally told ya what it was and ya basically laughed in my face."

"I didn't laugh, Nuccio."

"No, but your response did."

"Look, I'm not gonna lie. There's no cash in sports parks anymore. It's like being a farmer. They're all selling out to contractors. That's where the money is."

"It wouldn't be the same to me."

"Without profit, nothing takes off, Nuccio."

"I don't want any money from it."

Billy stops short. "Hold on, you're telling me you would do this for nothing?"

"It's not for nothing."

"Then what is it for?"

"I need to leave this earth knowin' I did somethin' good for once in my life." Ladro's comment from the hospital has stayed with Nutsy.

"So, in the end, this is about YOUR regrets, isn't it?"

Nutsy heats up a little. "I have no regrets, I do have wishes though."

"I'm confused… how is this gonna take care of N-J if it's not profitable?"

Nutsy stays quiet since he doesn't have an answer and Billy knows it.

"Yeah, I thought so… just consider a residential complex. It would be more guaranteed."

"Billy, I'm gonna say this right now. It's either a sports park or it's nothing."

"Well, then it looks like nothing to me."

"Yeah sure, we drive around in nice cars, do what we want when we want. What life does this kid have, ha? The one fuckin' thing he loved in life was taken from him at a young age."

"Jesus Christ, Nutsy, he has a good life. He has a better life than you and me. Who gives a fuck about all those things? Look at you. You have it all, but still look miserable."

"Yeah well, you should be in Naples fucking whoever ya can instead of worrying about all this. I'm gonna finish the game." Nutsy turns to head back toward his house.

"You wanna know why I'm still here?"

Nutsy turns and sarcastically replies, "Yeah, because ya gotta stick your nose up everyone's ass like a politician."

Billy storms over and gets in Nutsy's face, "I should kick your ungrateful ass up and down this street. If you weren't so fucking bull headed and listened to me, you would've been out of this shit a long time ago."

"Well, I'm not."

"No shit. You ain't the only one here with wishes and wants."

"I'm gonna finish watching the game." Nutsy turns back to head toward the house.

Billy yells out, "You're gonna blow this one shot you have because of your stubbornness!"

"Whatever!" Nutsy continues heading towards his house.

"Yeah whatever... don't come begging me for help, like you always do."

Nutsy turns. "Begging you?"

"That's right, begging. If it wasn't for me, you'd be mopping the streets for Squalo right now."

"Oh, so now you get all the credit for everything?"

"Just go watch your game. Hopefully, you don't get your ass handed to you like years ago."

Kathy heard the commotion from the house and is about where Nutsy is on the street and asks, "What the hell is going on? I hear you two all the way –"

"Ask the politician. He'll tell ya like he tells ya everything." Nutsy heads back toward his house.

Kathy asks Billy, "Is this really necessary between you two?"

"What is it with him? I mean, a sports park, come on."

"What sports park?" Kathy curiously asks.

"Don't you know? That's what he wants to turn that dump into."

"Ah… that's what his drawings are about."

"You can't let him try it, Kathy. You'll both be done for good… why do you think it's been sitting that way for years?"

CHAPTER 13

After Kathy and Billy finished their conversation, Billy heads back to his house. He wasn't in the mood to get into it with Nutsy any further, so he told Kathy that they would continue the discussion tomorrow.

Nutsy enters his living room where N-J and Sammy are both sitting on the couch. N-J is still embarrassed from earlier and thinks Nutsy is pissed off at him, so he tries to purposely not make eye contact with Nutsy.

Nutsy knows his son like a book and that N-J is purposely avoiding him. "N-J, come in the kitchen with me." Nutsy enters the kitchen and waits for N-J. After about a minute, N-J reluctantly enters the kitchen and Nutsy says, "Take a seat."

N-J takes a seat at the table with Nutsy and says, "You're mad at —"

"I'm not mad. I'm disappointed with your decision. Why would ya try that if ya know you can't swim?"

N-J looks away since he doesn't want to admit to the real reason, so Nutsy continues on, "I'm not leaving here without an answer."

N-J hesitantly replies, "I was trying to win that bet."

"Why though, if ya knew it was impossible?"

N-J turns since he doesn't want to admit to the truth. He feels his father might become more annoyed than he already is.

Nutsy heats up a bit and asks, "I asked ya why, God Dammit?"

A tear rolls down N-J's cheek since he can tell Nutsy is now truly aggravated with him. Nutsy knows his reaction startled N-J and softens his tone, "Alright... just tell me why ya tried it. It's all I wanna know."

Kathy is now listening in the foyer.

"You don't really wanna know, Papa."

"I do."

N-J blurts out, "Because there's no excitement at that place I live. All I do is stare at the TV and read magazines. My life is boring, that's why."

Nutsy sighs. All this time he thought his son was happy at the place he's living at. Maybe being preoccupied, Nutsy never saw the signs. "But ya have your friends there."

"I want my family... and you never come to visit me anymore." N-J turns away.

"Come on, I just brought ya a new glove, didn't I?"

"Yeah, last week and you haven't been back since then. Mom and grandpa come all the time."

"Do they bring ya anything?"

N-J finally explodes, "I don't want anything! I just want you to come visit me!"

Kathy wipes a tear rolling down her cheek.

"I'm sorry. Papa's been busy these days."

"What else is new? That's what you always say to me… and why can't I work with you? I'm good with numbers."

"Ya don't wanna do what I do, trust me."

"You just say that because you don't think I can… you always thought I was an idiot." N-J storms away.

Kathy steps up the staircase. She doesn't want N-J to know she was listening.

"N-J, get back here!" Nutsy yells out.

N-J continues out of the kitchen without turning back or responding. Nutsy's eyes close with disappointment and guilt. He knows he hasn't been around for N-J lately.

Nutsy jumps into his car and takes off down the street. He knows he's a complex man and doesn't do well with showing his true feelings. This comment from N-J hit him hard. He always thought N-J was happy and content, but now he knows N-J's true feelings.

He also knows he hasn't been around for N-J that much because of the current events that have consumed his time. This isn't how he hoped his life would turn out. He always wished for a close family after his father had passed away when he was young.

Nutsy always promised himself he would do anything to make sure his family stays tight. His relationship with N-J means the world to him. It's tough though, Nutsy always felt he had to act a certain way with N-J and couldn't be himself. N-J, on the other hand, always knew his father treated him differently but has never said anything until today. This has always bothered N-J, but he never wanted to disappoint his father so he kept it to himself.

Nutsy parks in front of a small cemetery on the east side by the New Row border. He walks toward a headstone. Every time he comes here, it reminds him of the first day he walked this path after his father's funeral. This is one reason he doesn't visit too often. It's not that he doesn't want to come, but the deep cut of how his father had dropped dead in front of him resurfaces and the pain emerges.

Nutsy was exceptionally close with his family from a young age. His father was a diehard baseball fan and Nutsy spent many nights watching games with him in their tiny apartment on a thirteen inch black and white TV. Many of Nutsy's friends already had color TVs but Nutsy didn't mind, it was the time he spent with his father that mattered to him. He can now realize how N-J feels.

Nutsy's father was a construction worker and dropped dead of a heart attack during a neighborhood feast one night. Nutsy never discusses it with anyone, but it's been a pain he's been carrying around for years. Nutsy had just gotten a bag of zeppoles with extra white powder. Both Nutsy and his father loved the extra white powder, his sister, not as much because it covered her lips and everyone would tease her.

From the day N-J was born, Nutsy promised he'd be around as long as he could for his family, but he's starting to feel pressure and tightness in his chest more often and he's becoming concerned. What if I have what my father had? Is it hereditary? Am I following in the same path as he did? These are all thoughts circling through his mind as he stands in front of his father's headstone that reads: In Loving Memory of Grazio Gento.

Nutsy takes in a deep breath. This is never easy for him. He gazes around and the vision of his father passing out right by his feet flashes through his mind. Nutsy then dropped his bag of zeppoles and frantically squatted down next to his father. His father had a massive heart attack and died instantly.

A random tear rolls down Nutsy's cheek. Not many things make him tear up, but this cut is still fresh to this very day. He peeks over toward a young lady and her daughter in the row next to him. She is about thirty-five and her daughter about eight.

The lady wipes her cheek with a tissue. Her daughter is playing with a doll and appears to be too young to know the impact of her father's death. The lady catches eyes with Nutsy and heads toward him since they know each other from the neighborhood.

She gives Nutsy a kiss on the cheek and he asks, "How's ya daughter doing?"

"She seems okay for the time being."

"How about, yourself?"

"I'm hanging in there the best I can. He never finished with the life insurance policy, so it's tough, Nutsy. But I'll be okay."

Her husband had gotten into a horrendous car accident and lost his life a few months ago. He was the neighborhood plumber and did many odd jobs for Nutsy.

"What do ya mean he never finished it?" Nutsy curiously asks.

"He applied but never completed the exam. I got a letter and his initial deposit back."

"Oh, I'm sorry to hear that. Ya know us guys, always running to nowhere."

"Yeah, it's just my luck."

So Nutsy takes a glimpse of the young girl. He can't help but think that was him years ago. He reaches into his pocket and pulls out a roll of cash and offers it to the lady. "Here, it's not much, but let me take care of the groceries for the month."

The lady takes a glimpse at the roll which appears much thicker than a month's worth of groceries. "How much is there?" she asks.

"It's two grand. Take it. Make sure you and your daughter eat good and stay strong."

"I can't take this from you. It's not right. You have your own family to worry about."

"Your husband always did right by me and never charged me full price... here, I insist, and I don't like to be told no."

The lady laughs and replies, "You've always been a good man, Nutsy. My husband always said you're a man with an armored shield and a soft heart underneath."

"Ah... what can I say... life sometimes takes us on a different journey... here, take it."

So the lady reluctantly takes the roll of cash and Nutsy continues on, "When ya need more, ya stop by my bar. I'll walk out with you. It's getting dark."

The lady and her daughter leave the cemetery with Nutsy and she catches him wiping away a tear while heading towards his car.

The fundraiser is over but everyone is still piled by the bar while watching the game. It's the fourth quarter and the score is 17-14, the Bears are winning. Since the total score of the game is now thirty-one, the under is still in play. There's about three minutes left in the game and Squalo couldn't be happier since the Bears have the ball and should just burn out the clock.

Ladro is intensely watching the game from his living room couch with his dog, Bandit, by his side. The new blue leather couch that Blackie had ordered a few weeks ago is causing Ladro to continuously slip down on it and he yells out, "This couch is driving me nuts."

Blackie enters the living room and asks, "What's wrong with it?"

"It's too slippery. I think they sprayed olive oil on it."

"Don't be ridiculous. Let's go to Scotties for dinner. I don't feel like cooking."

"Not now. There's only a few minutes left."

Ladro whips out his cell phone and calls Nutsy. Nutsy answers in his car, "You're still home, right?"

Ladro laughs and answers, "You watching this thing or what?"

"No."

"No? Where are you?"

"I had to stop off somewhere?"

"It's the fix of the year and you're not even watching it?"

"Nope."

"You feel alright?"

"I've felt better."

"What's wrong?"

"I don't know. My chest is tight… all I think about is when my father collapsed. I remember seeing him grabbing his chest a few weeks before he died."

"Ah, Nutsy, I know what you're thinking, but we never go down like each other."

"How do ya know?"

"Go home and have a glass of wine and relax."

"I just feel like my life is nothing that I ever planned it would be."

"Whose is?"

"We're not creators, we're takers. Ya know that, right?"

"Nutsy, we're bookmakers and provide entertainment to people who want it."

"No we don't. We take money from people who can't even afford to gamble. We don't help them." Nutsy pulls up in front of his house.

Ladro replies, "Nutsy, you're blessed with a beautiful family that loves you, never forget that."

"I just got home. I'll call ya later." Nutsy hangs up the call and gets out of his car.

Blackie wanders back into the living room and asks Ladro, "Was that my brother?"

"Yeah, he's been bringing up your father lately."

"He still hasn't gotten over that night... and I don't think he ever will."

"He harbors things, Blackie."

"He always did."

"I just got this email from the furniture store about a delivery coming next week. What's that about?"

"I ordered a new bedroom and dining room set."

"With what money?"

"The account in the wall," Blackie sarcastically replies and walks out.

"That's not all my money."

Blackie replies from the foyer, "Just be glad that's all I ordered."

Nutsy enters his living room where N-J and Sammy are sitting on the couch watching the end of the football game. N-J is glued to the TV and wants the over to hit so badly to prove to his father he knows what he's talking about.

Nutsy sits on a white club chair and gazes toward the TV. He doesn't even know which way to think at this point. Yes, he wants the over to hit and finally put this game to bed, but this really doesn't change much for him in the end. He's still a city bookmaker taking money from gamblers.

"Dad, we need two field goals and the over covers."

"The game is over, N-J. There's only a minute left. The Bears will burn out the clock."

"They can't, Papa. It's forth down."

"What?" At this point Nutsy hasn't been concentrating on the game but this finally sparks him up.

CHAPTER 14

Squalo, Leo, and Belo are still watching the football game at the bar in the catering hall. A bunch of other guests are scattered around them. Squalo's beaming and being his cocky self since the total score is thirty-one and even if the Bears hit this field goal, the under is still in play.

All eyes are now glued to the flat screen TV behind the bar as the Bears line up to kick a field goal. The center snaps the ball and the kicker boots it in the air. Squalo smiles because this doesn't really matter much to him whether it's good or not.

Ladro's eyes are glued to the TV. "Fuck! These shitheads in Vegas are the biggest thieves." He chucks his sandwich at the screen.

Blackie says from the kitchen, "I told you to watch your mouth and you better not be throwing anything."

N-J has an upset look on his face since the ball tailed off to the right and missed wide. "Wait. Is that a flag on the ground?" Sammy asks while pointing toward the screen.

Nutsy asks, "Where?"

"No," N-J replies with a disappointed tone.

"Look! The ref on the side is picking it up." Sammy points again toward the TV.

"Oh, shit, you're right," N-J replies and then covers his mouth after realizing what he had said.

Nutsy chuckles inside.

Squalo is now annoyed and barks out toward the TV, "This is bullshit. He wasn't off sides."

Belo replies, "It doesn't matter anyway whether he makes it or not."

"Until the clock shows zero, anything could happen," Squalo replies.

Nutsy's cell phone rings and he answers, "Ya watching?"

Ladro replies from his couch, "Imagine this shit? We'll still lose by a field goal anyway."

The Bears line up to kick another field goal. One of the refs throws his flag onto the field.

"Are ya kiddin' me?" Nutsy yells out.

Ladro replies, "I hate when they do that icing shit."

"Ya make it sound like a cupcake."

While still sitting at the bar, Squalo says, "They're icing his ass."

Leo replies, "Look at you guys. Fucking glued to a TV watching a bunch of guys that don't give a shit about you."

Squalo replies, "No one said we give a shit about them, it's the line we care about."

"Yeah, the line. You sound like a bunch of degenerates," Leo sarcastically replies.

Nutsy says to Ladro on the phone, "Do ya know how many eyes must be glued to this game right now?"

Ladro laughs and replies, "So, I guess this is entertaining after all, ha?"

"Don't be a smart-ass. Ya know exactly what I'm talkin' about."

"Yeah, but we'll never get this tingle anywhere else."

The Bears line back up at the ball after their huddle. The kicker takes a deep breath, nods to his setter. The center snaps the ball and Ladro yells out, "And here it is!"

As the kicker steps forward to boot the football, the defensive end dives fully extended toward the setter. The kicker boots the football and it deflects off the tip of the defensive end's fingers. The ball wobbles toward the side of the field.

"Dad, look, they got it!" N-J excitedly yells out.

"Where?" Nutsy's trying to follow all the commotion on the screen.

Ladro yells out, "Holy shit! He's flying down the sideline. Go you fucker!"

A Pac player that recovered the football is now sprinting toward the goal line.

Squalo hurls his whiskey glass against a wall. "Fuck this shit, where's the flag now God dammit?!"

Leo laughs at his father's behavior. "Yeah, a lock, ha?"

"Who fucking asked you?" Squalo snaps back.

A manager approaches the bar and says, "I'm sorry, everyone has to leave. I can't have this behavior here."

"We ain't going anywhere until this game is done," Squalo snaps back.

Leo replies, "You already lost. Let's get outta here."

The Pac player gets tackled on the two-yard line and then flops over the goal line.

Nutsy and N-J are now anxiously standing in front of the TV to see if the player scored or not and Sammy says, "Will you two move out of the way. I can't see anything."

Nutsy and N-J move off to the side. Nutsy still has Ladro on the phone and asks, "Was his knee down or not?"

"I don't know. They didn't give him the touchdown yet."

"Shit, ten seconds left… challenge it ya fuckin' moron."

Kathy can't watch but is listening from the kitchen and makes the sign of the cross. "Please let him win. I can't go through that again," she whispers to herself while gazing toward the ceiling.

The TV shows the replay in slow motion of the player being tackled but the angle is hard to see if his knee touched the ground before he fell over the goal line.

"Shit… it's hard to tell if he crossed," Nutsy says.

Munchie stands by the TV in his living room shitting a brick. Although he heavily bet the under, he knows Nutsy is returning the money to him if it hits, so he's rooting for the over. It sounds crazy, but Munchie doesn't want to have to explain to Squalo that their wagers were not booked if they won.

Nutsy peeks at his phone and says to Ladro, "I'll call ya right back. It's Binky." So Nutsy clicks his phone and asks, "You watching or what?"

"You bet your ass I am."

Nutsy peeks over toward N-J and replies, "My kid called it."

"What? The over?"

"Yup, and the Pac."

"Shit, I'll hire him as my handicapper." Binky laughs.

After the review, a ref raises both hands up in the air and N-J excitedly leaps up. "Yes!"

Binky says, "Sleep tight, and not like our other friend."

"What about him?"

"We'll talk tomorrow."

Kathy enters the living room after hearing N-J's loud cheer from the touchdown. "It sounds like it's a good game." Although she doesn't follow football, she knows damn well how the point spread works and that the over has hit.

N-J blurts out, "Mom, not good, it's great. Both my bets won."

Kathy turns toward Nutsy and asks, "You let him bet?"

"Leave 'im alone, he's having fun right now."

"I was right, ma. I told Papa what would hit."

"Just great, now he's even starting to sound like you," Kathy says to Nutsy.

Sammy says, "It's only for one game, ma."

"Yeah, and that's how it starts." Kathy's not thrilled with N-J even thinking about gambling.

Although Nutsy already hit the over bet, he wants N-J to feel good about the game and have fun for once. "We're not out of the woods yet," Nutsy says since N-J also wants the Packers to win.

"How can we lose?" N-J asks.

Kathy asks, "Really now?"

"This is fun, ma. It's better than sitting in that room all day."

Kathy gives Nutsy an annoyed look and asks, "Do you see what you're doing?"

So Nutsy ignores Kathy's question and gets back to N-J's original question and replies, "There's still a chance of a Bears runback."

Kathy's eyes roll while she walks out.

Munchie is ecstatic that the over covered. At least now he won't have any issues with Squalo. He would rather at this point take a loss than tell Squalo his bets never got booked.

Squalo storms out of the catering hall toward his car in the parking lot. Leo hobbles behind him but makes sure to take his time. He finds it hysterical the way his father is acting because of a football game. Up to this point, he knows about the game apparently being fixed, but he doesn't have a clue about Squalo pushing his client's under bets onto Nutsy.

Leo finally gets into Squalo's car and asks, "I'm not getting this. Didn't most people bet the under?"

Squalo hits the gas and replies, "Yeah."

"I'm no gambler, but I'm thinking you should be excited to be a bookmaker right now."

Squalo ignores Leo's comment and continues to drive away. So Leo asks, "Did you hear me?"

Squalo snaps back, "Yup… we dumped the majority of our under bets onto Nutsy?"

Leo has no idea what Squalo is saying and asks, "What are you talking about?"

"We wanted him to eat them."

"Hold on… you're telling me you gave Nutsy all your under bets?"

Squalo nods yes and replies, "Munchie called them in under his code."

"Why Munchie?"

"Same reason you're pressuring him… because we can."

Leo bursts out in laughter and Squalo barks out, "Yeah, real fucking funny, isn't it?"

"You better pack it up, old man. The shark's losing its instincts. How much are we talking here?"

"Over a half."

"Mill?"

While Squalo just nods, Leo breaks out in laughter again. Squalo's burning up inside and spins the wheel. "Where are you going?" Leo asks.

"To the rodent's apartment. I'm surprised he hasn't called yet."

Squalo bangs on Donnola's front door and impatiently waits. He bangs again a few more times. "Open up!" Squalo whips out his cell phone and calls Donnola. Since Donnola didn't answer, Squalo bangs again and yells, "Stop pulling it and answer, will ya?"

Leo waits in the car for Squalo to return from Donnola's place and makes a call. Miguel is now at his two story brick house in the Bronx overlooking the Long Island Sound and answers his cell phone from a large deck off the back of the house, "What's up, Lion?"

"Your guy, is he still into arms or what?"

"I think a little… but he moved into trafficking. That's where the money is today."

"Fuck that. I want no part of that shit. Set up a meeting. I wanna talk to him."

"I'll see what I can do. He's big now and doesn't communicate on a street level."

"You tell him The Lion's out and wants to talk." Leo hangs up.

CHAPTER 15

The next afternoon, Nutsy meets with Binky at his Italian Restaurant on Arthur Avenue. It's smack in the middle of the block and surrounded by bakeries, Italian delis, pizza shops, and other restaurants, mainly Italian. The block is known for their homemade recipes and many patrons travel great distances for the experience and the history.

Nutsy and Binky are now in the back of the restaurant having a late lunch. It's modern but still has old world charm since the inside has brick walls and floor to ceiling wooden wine racks. Binky knows Nutsy loves Eggplant Rollatini and had his chef make it for him. Nutsy is devouring it and Binky sarcastically says, "Whoa, slow down. I'm not charging you."

Nutsy laughs and replies, "I gotta say, you're right. This is fantastic."

"I told you, didn't I?"

Nutsy swallows the last bite, wipes his mouth with a napkin, and says, "Alright, I enjoyed that. Let's finish our conversation from before."

"When's this all happening?" Binky asks.

"I don't know yet. I'm still tryin' to figure out a way to make it work."

"Does Papo know this?"

"No one does, not even Ladro."

Nutsy turns and notices Belo approaching the table. He agreed to allow Belo to join them, but doesn't really know why Binky insisted as of yet.

So Belo stands by the table and nods to the both of them and waits. Belo's being respectful and waiting for Nutsy to agree. Nutsy and Belo catch eyes and Nutsy gives his nod since he feels he at least owes Belo this much after saving his son's life.

Belo takes a seat and Nutsy says, "You were the only one out of the group that even came to the water, let alone helped my son."

"Business is one thing. Our families are another," Belo replies.

Binky raises his espresso cup and says, "Amen to that."

"Look, Nutsy, I swear I will never cross you again. We were just taking a beating and thought you'd give in a little."

Binky laughs and cuts in, "Who, this fucking bull-headed mule? You should've known better than that."

"Well, that's why I didn't push my bets onto you like the other two did."

Binky appears confused and asks, "They did what?"

Belo replies, "They used one of Nutsy's clients to push their under bets on him, so he would eat them."

Binky's eyes open wide and he asks, "So you booked all of Squalo and Donnola's under bets?"

Nutsy smiles and nods yes.

"Jesus Christ… how much are we talking here?" Binky curiously asks.

"Enough… let's leave it at that."

Belo replies, "Squalo was sick leaving that place. I guarantee you, he had diarrhea all night."

Nutsy asks Binky, "So why did ya ask Belo to come?" Nutsy's still curious about why Binky insisted Belo come meet them.

"I'm thinking if this works out, I'll take the east side since I'm closer to the water and he can have the west. We can split the city in half."

Nutsy leans back to think it over. He feels like he owes Belo but is not sure of this scenario presented to him. "Why wouldn't ya take it all?" Nutsy hesitantly asks Binky.

"The older you get the more you realize it's better to spread it around than try and keep it all. Besides, I don't like the west side of your city. It's too industrial for me."

"Partners are not always the greatest thing either," Nutsy replies.

"You suffered in that basement for a long time when you had no help, remember?" Binky asks.

"Ain't that the truth? I ate tuna fish for months and can still taste it."

Belo asks, "Why would you wanna get out anyway? You have a good thing going."

"I gave my word to Billy if this works out… but it's only if it does. Ya two understand that, right?"

Belo nods in agreement and asks, "Does Ladro know this?"

Nutsy shakes his head no.

Belo says, "He ain't gonna go for this. He's been with you from the start."

"If I get out so does he. He'll have no choice."

Binky replies, "You say that now but –"

"We should be more concerned about Belo and the stooges than worried about Ladro."

Belo replies, "One of the stooges won't be anyone's concern anymore."

Nutsy asks, "What do ya mean?"

Binky cuts in, "Let's just say we always thought alike, and Belo needed to prove himself again."

Nutsy glances back and forth toward the both of them. He has an idea what Binky's saying, but remains quiet.

After their discussion was finished in the restaurant, the three of them take a ten block stroll heading west. The streets change quickly in this part of the city, but Binky needed to stop into a store to collect. He figures Nutsy and Belo could use some exercise after the heavy lunch they all ate and having them around gives him some extra security.

"It's still rough around here, ha?" Nutsy whispers.

Binky nods yes as they now pass a few derelicts hanging out on a street corner. Nutsy spots one of them opening his jacket and placing his hand inside.

An SUV pulls up on the corner with tinted windows and the back window slowly opens, but only about a quarter of the way. The tip of a pistol sticks out from the window and Nutsy notices the derelict on the corner whipping out a pistol. "Get down!" Nutsy yells out.

They all hit the deck while the derelicts exchange gun fire with the SUV. Nutsy, Binky, and Belo anxiously crawl to a spot behind a parked car and wait. They all have pistols drawn.

The SUV peels out and heads down the street. One of the derelicts is sprawled out on the ground. There's complete chaos and screams on the street with pedestrians taking cover or attempting to bolt away.

Binky asks while they all squat behind the parked car, "Are you two alright?"

While Belo nods yes, Nutsy grimaces in pain.

"You got hit?" Binky asks.

"In the shoulder," Nutsy replies.

"You want me to call an ambulance?" Binky asks.

"No, I'll deal with it on my own."

"Do you guys have permits for this city?" Binky asks.

Both Nutsy and Belo shake their heads no.

"Alright… let's get outta here. You'll both be fucked down here with those things."

They all stand up and head in the opposite direction.

"I swear, Nutsy, these punks need to be taught a lesson," Binky angrily says.

Squalo pulls up in front of the body shop after running a few errands with Leo. Belinda had already closed the shop for the day. Leo squirms out of the passenger seat and asks, "You smell that?"

Squalo replies while still sitting in the driver's seat, "No. Hurry up. I wanna get home."

While Leo hobbles toward the entrance, Squalo dials Donnola again and waits for him to answer. After about twenty seconds he hangs up. "What the hell is this asshole doing?" he mumbles to himself.

Leo stands in the lobby and notices a distinct smell coming from the room Belinda had thrown a lit rag in. He opens the door and sees the room roaring in flames. "What the fuck?!"

Leo quickly bolts outside as fast as he can regardless of his foot and yells to Squalo, "Call the fire department!"

"Why?"

"Just fucking call them!"

Nutsy heads back toward his city. What a fucking lunch he thinks to himself. At least the Eggplant was good. He calls Munchie and waits for him to answer.

Munchie and Belinda are in Munchie's house getting ready to go out to dinner. Belinda notices Nuccio displaying on his cell phone and hands the phone off to Munchie. "Here, it's Nutsy."

"What does he want now? He already cleaned me out."

"You? I can't believe you talked me into that bet."

"You're the one who asked me about it, remember?"

"You told me it was guaranteed."

Munchie shrugs it off and answers the phone, "I have no bets for you."

"Where are ya?" Nutsy asks.

"Home why?"

"I need to meet ya at your office."

"How come?"

"I'll meet ya there in ten minutes." Nutsy hangs up.

Squalo and Leo stand in front of the shop while watching flames engulf the structure. They both can't believe it. A fire truck storms down the street with its sirens blaring. The truck pulls up near the front of the building and the firefighters anxiously hop off the truck and get to work.

Munchie is ready to leave his house and Belinda asks, "What did he want?"

"Who knows? It's always a surprise."

Belinda's cell phone rings and she answers, "What, Leo?"

Leo is steaming on the other end. "What the hell did you do? The building's on fire!"

Belinda tries to seem surprised. "What? I'll be right there."

"Don't even bother. There's nothing to see anymore," Leo replies.

Belinda hangs up and Munchie asks, "What's wrong?"

"I can't believe it. My brother said the store's on fire."

"Let's go. I'll bring you there."

"No, I'll go. You meet Nutsy."

After meeting up at Munchie's office, Nutsy and Munchie head toward an examining room. "How did this happen?" Munchie asks.

"I got caught in a shootout downtown."

They enter the examining room and Nutsy removes his jacket and shirt. His shoulder is now covered in blood. "Shit, you did get hit. You don't feel it?"

"Of course I do."

"Well, at least it hit a meaty spot. You need to go to the hospital for this."

"No, you're gonna take it out."

"No way. I'm not taking this out."

"Go grab your pliers or whatever the fuck ya call 'em."

"Nutsy, this needs to be done correctly. Remember when your other shoulder got sliced open and you wouldn't go to the hospital?"

"Yeah, I remember."

"You had a high fever for weeks after it got badly infected."

"Shut the fuck up and go get your pliers."

Munchie shakes his head and pulls open a drawer from a cabinet. He removes a pair of clippers, medicine tape, and gauze. "This is ridiculous. I'm telling you now, I'm not responsible if this doesn't work out."

"Yank it out already, will ya." Nutsy doesn't have any patience for the back and forth.

Munchie dabs a cloth with rubbing alcohol and pats the bloody hole. Nutsy snatches the bottle out of Munchie's hand and pours it over his shoulder. "Ah, fuck!" Nutsy yells out.

"I was trying to avoid that."

"You're wiping it like it's a baby ass." Nutsy pours more over his shoulder and winces in pain. "Alright, dig it out."

"Nutsy, this –"

"Get me a fuckin' towel."

Munchie hands him a towel and Nutsy says, "Do it." Nutsy bites down hard onto the towel.

Munchie sighs and starts gently picking at the wound.

Nutsy removes the towel from his mouth and says, "Stop fuckin' playing with it and dig it out."

"Okay." So Munchie digs into the hole with the clippers. Nutsy bites onto the towel again and turns his head.

"Are you okay," Munchie asks.

Nutsy nods yes and Munchie continues to dig away.

The body shop is now completely charred. The flames are contained but the structure is a burned pile of rubble with smoldering ashes. Leo is steaming inside. He was excited to take the shop back over from Belinda and start his illegal enterprise again from it.

Munchie's still digging away into Nutsy's shoulder. "Jesus Christ. Did ya find it yet?" Nutsy impatiently asks.

"I got it, but it's sideways. I'm trying to turn it so it doesn't cause any more damage. This should be done in the hospital, not here."

"Just keep digging. What does it look like?"

"Maybe, a twenty-two."

"Good, yank it out."

"I'm trying."

Nutsy knows Munchie is somewhat timid and attempts to wind him up with some insulting comments. "Ya know something, you've always been half a man."

"What?"

"You heard me. Yeah, I heard Belinda's falling asleep."

"I don't appreciate what you're saying."

"Yeah, I heard ya can't even get it up."

"Who told you that?" It's been the truth, so Munchie doesn't know that Nutsy's just breaking horns and his comments are a coincidence.

"Are ya kidding? Everyone knows… imagine that shit, a doctor who can't get it up?"

"Fuck you, Nutsy… you want me to yank this out? I'll yank it sideways if I have to." Munchie is annoyed.

"No, I gotta better idea. How about ya rub my balls, ya fuckin' half a man."

"That's it!" Munchie digs deeper into Nutsy's shoulder. Nutsy bites down hard onto the towel since he knows he has Munchie finally wound up. Sweat is pouring down both of their faces while Munchie continues to dig deeper.

Nutsy turns his head and bites harder onto the towel since the pain is excruciating. His face turns pale while sweat now pours off of his cheeks. Munchie clamps down onto the bullet and says, "You better bite harder." Munchie forcefully attempts to pull the bullet out but it's lodged.

"Yank it! Ya fuckin' half a man!" Nutsy yells out.

So Munchie yanks on the clippers with all his might and the bullet finally dislodges and comes out of Nutsy's shoulder. "Holy shit. I did it!" Munchie's ecstatic he was able to complete this task. It's the first bullet he ever removed in his office with clippers.

Nutsy's still glaring at the wall. His face is completely covered in sweat and he's pale as a ghost, almost in complete shock.

"Nutsy, you okay?" Munchie asks.

Nutsy doesn't respond. He's completely in another world. "Nutsy!" Munchie yells out.

Nutsy finally snaps out of his daze and says, "Ya fuckin' did it, ya mamaluke. What was it?"

"It looks like twenty-two range ammo to me."

"Shit, I could only imagine a hollow point. Alright, stitch it."

Munchie takes a glimpse of the hole in Nutsy's shoulder and replies, "Let the hospital do this. You'll need over thirty stitches for this."

"Go get the thread and the needle."

"Nutsy, come on. This is ridiculous."

"The hard part's over, go get it."

Munchie can't believe this is happening and just stares at Nutsy.

"Go get it! And bring me back a bottle of liquor."

"I don't have liquor in here."

"Bullshit!"

So Munchie heads toward the door and replies, "There's something seriously wrong with you."

Nutsy laughs and replies, "You can stick this scene in your book one day." Nutsy takes a peek at the hole. Blood pours down his shoulder, so he wipes it off with the towel he's been holding. He can really see the nasty hole in his shoulder now. "Shit, now my other shoulder's fucked up."

Munchie enters the room with a bottle of scotch, a needle, and thread. "How did this happen?"

"Right in broad daylight on a street corner. Imagine that shit?"

"You should know better, the city's like a war zone."

Nutsy takes the bottle from Munchie and says, "Get me a clean towel." He wipes his shoulder again and chucks the towel onto the floor.

Munchie hands off a fresh towel to Nutsy and says, "Don't throw it on the floor."

So Nutsy rolls his eyes, bites down on the clean towel, and pours the scotch onto his shoulder. "Ya sister's ass!" Nutsy yells out and pours more onto his shoulder.

CHAPTER 16

After witnessing the destruction of the shop with her own eyes, Belinda passes by Blackie's bank and notices her office light still on. Belinda bangs on the front door and Blackie unlocks it to let her in. Belinda walks in and without hesitation says, "It's down to the ground… when can I start?"

"I don't believe you."

"I told you I'd do anything to not be associated with either of them anymore."

"Wow, you really did it?"

Belinda nods yes and asks again, "So, when can I start?"

"As long as you're not bullshitting me, when the papers are completed, and you're cleared through compliance." Blackie opens a drawer and pulls out a file. She hands off a few stapled papers to Belinda.

"I'll be looking forward to it." Belinda heads out of the office but turns and says, "Your brother taught you well."

"I'm not following you."

"In the old days, you would've done this yourself. Now you're using your head to get the same results."

While Munchie threads stitches through Nutsy's shoulder, he asks, "Did you really mean what you said earlier?"

So Nutsy takes a swig from the bottle and laughs. "Nah, I was just playin' with ya so you'd get the job done."

"You're a character. You know that, Nutsy?"

"Who knows, maybe one day someone will make a movie about my life."

"That would be an interesting movie, I gotta say."

"We'll even make the potato chip eating doctor who can't get it up, a character."

"Here we go again."

Nutsy takes another swig and says, "Alright, now to business. What the fuck were ya thinkin' about siding with the stooges?"

"I know it was stupid, but he threatened me."

"Who?"

"Squalo."

"How?" Nutsy takes another swig from the bottle.

"I don't know how he knew, but it was about my student loans I haven't paid."

"And ya bought it?"

"Nutsy, I can't afford any bad publicity like you guys can."

"What the hell is that supposed to mean?"

"You know what I mean." Munchie pulls the last thread through the hole. "I think we're done."

Nutsy hops off the examining table and says, "Ya did good, Doc... how much of the under bet was yours?"

"I wagered fifty on the under, but I also put ten on the Bears."

"Ya bet fifty-grand on a rumor? Ya really are a fuckin' moron... come see me tomorrow."

Munchie applies a white bandage over the stitches and hesitantly replies, "Belinda bet ten herself. She's been breaking my horns now."

"Good, ya deserve it." Nutsy heads toward the door.

"Hold on. I have to tape it."

Nutsy turns back and Munchie applies a few pieces of tape across the bandage. "I'm sorry about everything, Nutsy."

"Yeah, everyone's always sorry after the fact," Nutsy replies while heading toward the door to leave.

Squalo and Leo are now heading back to Squalo's apartment. Leo's livid and believes his place was purposely torched. "You know it was probably that cocksucker Ladro who did this," Leo says with an annoyed look on his face.

"It could be," Squalo replies but is short.

"It's like you don't seem to care."

"Why, you give a shit that I lost the bet?"

"You can't even compare the two. This is a business that burnt down."

"You know something, fuck your business. All I hear about are YOUR problems since you got out... what about mine?"

Leo firmly braces his hand on the dashboard and yells, "Watch out!"

So Squalo nervously spins the wheel and says, "I'm fine... stop yelling from the passenger seat, will you?"

"Let me drive. I don't think you can see anymore."

"You don't have a license, remember?"

"I'd rather take a chance with no license than sit in the car with you driving."

"Take a fucking bus then."

So Leo laughs it off and asks, "Who handles the insurance for the shop anyway?"

"Presto still has it."

"I thought he croaked?"

"He did, the son took it over."

"Great, that moron? He thought his shit didn't stink... you got his number?"

Squalo nods yes.

"Call him."

Squalo presses a button on the dashboard.

Presto is in his unfinished basement watching his son hit off of a baseball tee into a net. "I said, keep your head down."

Michael rolls his eyes and replies, "I am."

"You're not. I'm watching –"

Presto's cell phone rings and he answers, "Presto."

"Yeah, Presto, this is Leo."

"The Lion?"

"That's right."

Presto takes a glimpse at his cell phone display and asks, "How are you calling from your father's number?"

"I'm out."

"From jail?" Presto never cared for Leo either from back in the old neighborhood.

"No, from the bakery. We need to put a claim in. The shop burnt down."

"Belinda's shop?"

"It was always my shop. You still insure it, right?"

"Not anymore. Your father held off on the payment."

Squalo cuts in, "Whoa, wait a minute. You were supposed to shop around for a lower rate, remember?"

"Yeah, and I told you I didn't have anything better so you hung up on me."

"That didn't mean I wanted to cancel –"

Leo cuts in, "Are you telling me there's no insurance on this place?"

"I don't think the premium was ever paid." Presto knows damn well the premium wasn't paid and the policy is currently cancelled.

"Why didn't YOU fucking pay it then?" Leo heats up.

"Leo, it's not my responsibility to pay the premium."

"Oh, now you're forgetting the little people down here who started your father off? We'll finish this tomorrow." Leo hangs up the call and asks Squalo, "Why didn't you pay the premium?"

"Don't blame this on me… this asshole was supposed to find a better rate."

"He said he couldn't."

"Yeah, now he says it. That's very convenient."

"You should've moved the account after his father died… I never cared for this guy with his fake rope chains and Guido hairdo."

Nutsy enters his bedroom and removes his shirt. His shoulder is now completely bandaged up, with blood stains seeping through. Munchie had told him it would be normal to still see some blood stains for a while, and that he needs to change the bandage a few times a day.

While Nutsy chucks the bloody stained shirt into a garbage pail, Kathy enters the room and notices the bandage on his shoulder and asks, "What the hell happened to you?"

"Ah, nothing… I cut myself."

"Cut yourself? I would say that looks like more than a cut."

"Yeah, maybe just a little." Nutsy puts on a new shirt and enters the bathroom.

Kathy lifts the shirt out from the garbage pail. "Holy shit! What did you cut yourself on, a chain saw?"

N-J enters the bedroom and says, "Dad, I've been looking for you. The lines opened up for the weekend."

Nutsy replies from the bathroom, "N-J, this bet was for one game and one game only… don't even think about it anymore."

"But I'm good at it. Can't you tell?" N-J's seeking his father's approval.

Kathy's eyes close. She was always concerned about her son enjoying gambling just like her husband does.

"I have an idea. How about ya stay through Columbus Day weekend?" Nutsy asks N-J and attempts to change the topic.

"I would love that. Can I, ma?" N-J excitedly asks.

"Only, if there's no gambling."

"Of course not." Nutsy heads out of the room and down the staircase. He makes his way into the living room where Sammy sits on the couch with the ice pack still on her ankle.

"Dad, this isn't getting any better."

"Sprains take a long time."

"How do I know it's not broken?"

"Nah, you'd know. Trust me."

"Well, it really hurts, and I can't put any pressure on it at all."

The doorbell buzzes and Nutsy answers the front door and sees Bono standing by the entrance. "Hi, Mr. Gento." Bono offers his hand for a handshake.

Nutsy shakes Bono's hand and grimaces from the pain in his left shoulder. "She's in the living room."

While Bono heads toward the living room, he can't help but think about the first time he ever offered his hand and Nutsy was hesitant to shake it. Maybe he likes me now, Bono thinks. He shook my hand right away.

Nutsy hasn't formerly thanked Bono for saving N-J's life and takes this opportunity to do so. "That was a brave thing you did. I can't thank you enough."

Bono gleams since he finally received some satisfaction from Nutsy. N-J quickly darts toward Bono and hugs him with all his might. "You saved my life, Bono."

"No, I didn't. Your father did."

"You got to him first," Sammy replies with a smile.

So Nutsy peeks toward Sammy. He can tell by the sparkle in her eyes the affection she has toward Bono. Nutsy's been fighting his feelings all this time but finally asks Bono, "Why don't ya stay for dinner?"

Bono and Sammy catch eyes and she smiles with a nod for Bono to accept. "I'd love to, Mr. Gento. Thank you for asking me."

"Alright, listen… ya seem to be a respectful young man, but ya don't have to thank me all the time I ask ya something."

Bono nods and smiles. He knows he's been trying to be extra polite.

CHAPTER 17

A few days have passed and Nutsy and Ladro are up to the same routine at The Headquarters. They have decided to leave the money from Squalo's safe in Ladro's hiding spot for the time being. Nutsy did decide to return Munchie and Belinda's wagers for Munchie's services.

Ladro wasn't too thrilled with his decision and believed Nutsy should have returned five grand, at most. Nutsy had a change of heart and thought that his luck has been changing for the better since the underbet luckily went his way. The last time there was a rumor about a fixed game, Nutsy was ruined for years.

Nutsy knows things are starting to heat up around town and has been asked in a roundabout way to assist in cleaning them up. He has much more on the line today than years ago. An event like the past that he was involved with, could land him behind bars for the rest of his life. He's caught in the middle and feels the pressure of maintaining his fierce reputation from the past.

If he flat out declines, Nutsy knows his reputation will become tarnished and any up-and-coming wannabe or current operator will walk all over him. He feels he needs to be smarter about how he handles events moving forward. Luckily, he hasn't had to really think about any major situations for a while, but times are different today, and he senses it.

Nutsy might not be the most educated person on paper, but his intuition and instincts are second to none. He has a superb vision to assume when he can push the envelope and when he shouldn't. This makes him extremely difficult to figure out. Even his family and Ladro sometimes can't and it's because everything is based on a hunch, a gut feeling as some will call it.

N-J has been staying home for the week and Sammy is still nursing her sprained ankle. The swelling is slowly going down, but she's still not able to walk on it and has to use crutches while in school.

Kathy did finally decide to take Sammy to the hospital to get her ankle examined. The hospital took x-rays and performed a few other tests. Luckily, everything came back negative. The doctor on shift did mention it was a severe sprain and could take longer to heel than a break. The doctor said she could be on crutches for about a month's time.

Sammy is not thrilled with this one bit since she wanted to spend more time with Bono being out and about instead of being stuck in the house watching TV with him. In any case, they seem to be just as happy spending time together regardless of where it is.

Kathy has been enjoying her week off from work with N-J since Carmela took a flight back home to Florida and couldn't watch him. It's been a while since N-J had spent this much time at the house and it's making her think differently. One thing she would love, is to leave her job to care for him at home. She never considered this idea before since she always carried the family's health benefits and was concerned about a steady paycheck coming into the household.

Squalo and Leo haven't been getting along at all. Squalo told him to find his own place by the end of the month. Leo asked him how that was possible since the shop was burned down and they are still fighting with the insurance company. Squalo told him that wasn't his problem and to figure it out because he can't stay with him any longer.

Belinda is excited and ready for her new beginning at the bank with Blackie. Blackie was a little hesitant from the start to find Belinda a job, but she figured she's trying to move on with her life. Blackie remembers when she was trying to move forward as well. It's a huge adjustment and Blackie knows Belinda will never get support from her father or brother. In any case, since Belinda had torched the shop, Blackie feels Belinda had proved herself to her.

It's early Thursday morning and Leo sits in a local diner in The Plains with his father. They are trying to figure out their situation with the shop. Leo comes up with an idea and says, "This is what we'll do. We'll tell the insurance company you gave Presto cash."

"That's ridiculous."

"You know how these big companies are. They don't want the attention."

"So you want me to lie and say I gave him eight grand in what, a brown paper bag?"

"Why, will this be the first time you ever bullshitted anyone?"

"If it was that easy, everyone would do it."

"It's worth a shot. Call the company."

"It's your shop. You call."

Nutsy is getting ready to head up to the baseball facility. He's brushing his teeth when Kathy enters and remains uncharacteristically quiet. Nutsy notices and asks, "What happened to you, slept on the wrong side of the bed?"

"No." She brushes her hair and keeps it short.

"What? What did I do now?" Nutsy assumes he did something again to annoy her.

Kathy replies, "I'm thinking of leaving my job so N-J can stay home with us for good."

Nutsy washes his mouth out with water and then asks, "Ya heard my conversation with N-J the other day, didn't ya?"

Kathy nods yes with a disappointed look.

Nutsy pecks her on the lips and asks, "You'll never stop being a mother, will ya?"

"Never… so, what do you think?"

"It might be a good idea."

"What about the benefits?"

"We're both adults, I'm sure we can figure somethin' out."

Kathy perks up since she assumed Nutsy would never agree to it. "Wow, this is a first."

"Ya know me, I'm always full of surprises. We'll talk later when I get back."

Nutsy and Ladro are heading north on the Sprain Parkway in Ladro's car. They are on their way to meet Presto at the Columbus Day weekend tournament which is being held at the new baseball facility Presto invited Nutsy to. The facility is approximately an hour away and Ladro is becoming impatient while driving since he rarely ventures out more than fifteen minutes from his house. "Jesus Christ. This is like another fucking world."

"It seems that way, doesn't it?"

"Look over there, cows and horses. Where are you bringing me?" The open land on the side of the parkway is filled with cows and has a dilapidated barn.

Nutsy laughs and replies, "We've been stuck in four square miles for our entire lives. This is a nice change for once."

"You look like you're enjoying this."

"My mind feels relaxed looking at all this land. It seems peaceful up here."

"Peaceful? It looks depressing if you ask me… oh, shit!" Ladro spins the wheel. "Look at this curve. Couldn't they at least make the parkway straight?"

"Will ya just fuckin' drive and pay attention."

Leo finally finds the phone number to the insurance company. While still sitting in the diner with his father, Leo dials the number and impatiently waits for a claim representative to answer. One finally answers and Leo explains his situation. The claim rep took all of Leo's information down and explained the policy is currently cancelled.

"That's impossible. My father gave the broker the cash," Leo barks out.

The rep replies, "I don't see any deposits under the policy, sir."

"We can't control what he does with the cash… maybe he pocketed it."

"Our brokers don't act in that matter, sir."

"Well, something has to be done. My building is in ashes right now and the broker is holding eight grand of our cash."

"We would have to set up an investigation to look into this further."

"You do that. I'll be waiting." Leo hangs up.

"It's a waste of time," Squalo says.

"You just go along with the story," Leo replies.

Nutsy and Ladro stop off at a rest area a little more than halfway to the complex since they both need to use the restroom. "Imagine doing this commute. I think I'd have to wrap it with a rubber band," Ladro sarcastically says.

After going to the bathroom, they both leave the rest stop with a cup of coffee and hop back into the car. "Do me a favor, don't ask me to take a ride up here ever again," Ladro says.

Nutsy laughs while Ladro takes a sip from his coffee container and spits it out. "Even the coffee tastes like shit."

"It's the water."

"Yeah, they're probably getting it from a swamp or some shit like that."

"Am I gonna have to listen to this all day?"

"Probably... how much longer?"

Nutsy peeks at his watch and replies, "I don't know, maybe twenty minutes."

"Wonderful."

Squalo has enough of listening to Leo in the diner and says, "Let's get outta here. I got a headache listening to your bullshit."

"Yeah, you're just annoyed because Nutsy stuck it up your ass this weekend."

Squalo spots Miguel and a shady looking man heading toward their table and asks, "What's he doing here?"

Leo turns and replies, "I invited them. I gotta make money somehow. You ain't helping me out with shit."

Miguel and the shady man take a seat. Leo dealt with this guy before in the past but his business has grown tremendously and so has his attitude. "I don't have that much time… what can I do for you?" the man asks.

Leo replies, "What can you do for me? Wow, that's some welcome back."

"You think you're the only one who gets stuffed in the can and gets out? Talk, I gotta be somewhere in a half hour."

So Leo becomes a little irritated by the man's attitude and says, "Little Charlie, all big now, ha?"

"They call me Big Charlie now. Make sure you understand that."

"Is that right?"

"Yeah, that's right."

Miguel cuts in. He can tell this meeting isn't starting on the right foot. "Can we just do this? I need to get back for a meeting."

Leo and Big Charlie catch eyes. "So?" Big Charlie asks with an attitude.

"I'm looking for the most popular pistol on the street today."

"I'm going to the bathroom," Squalo says and heads toward the restroom. He wants no part of what's going on.

"What's his problem?" Big Charlie asks.

"He's got a bladder problem… so what is it?" Leo knows his father wants no part in this, but he can't let Big Charlie know that.

"It's the 9mm subcompact."

"What are they running?"

"Figure about a grand each."

"What? They're online for five hundred."

"Then buy them online." Big Charlie glances at Miguel and says, "Let's go. This is a waste of my time. This guy's got nothing now."

"I'll give you six."

Big Charlie stands up and says, "Nine. You let me know when you're ready."

"I think you're forgetting I was your biggest customer back in the day. I MADE Little Charlie who he is."

"That, my friend, was another lifetime ago." Big Charlie heads toward the exit. Miguel shrugs it off and follows him out.

Leo mumbles, "See? Everyone forgets who got them where they are. We'll see about this one."

Ladro and Nutsy are heading down a windy, wooded two lane road that's covered with red, yellow, and orange leaves. "Look at this, it's beautiful," Nutsy says while gazing out of the window.

"Oh, now you're a nature lover?"

"I always did enjoy different scenery."

"Do me a favor, let's get in and get the fuck home. This is like some spooky shit up here."

"Are ya kidding? This is where all the city people come to relax."

"You'll never catch me dead up here."

A deer darts across the road in front of their car and Ladro nervously spins the steering wheel while slamming on the brakes. "What the fuck!" Nutsy yells out as he lunges forward.

Their car swerves toward the side of the road and stops short on a grassy area. A few more deer dart across the road and Ladro sarcastically asks, "Yeah, relax, ha?"

"Where the fuck did they come from?" Nutsy's breathing heavily.

"It's hunting season, isn't it?"

"How the hell do I know? I've never hunted in my life."

"This is great. We'll be like Pesce in that movie when his wheels kept spinning in the mud."

"The only difference is I'll be stuck with you, not his girlfriend," Nutsy sarcastically replies.

"I wouldn't mind being stuck with her."

"Yeah, I'm sure ya wouldn't. Hit the gas, will ya? We're running late."

CHAPTER 18

Watching carefully to avoid any more deer darting across the wooded road, Ladro slowly hits the gas and the tire spins on the wet, muddy grass. "Shit!" Ladro yells out.

"Just fuckin' great… rock it back and forth."

"What do you mean, rock it?"

"Do I have to explain everything? Go a little backwards and a little forward."

So Ladro puts the car in reverse and it moves backwards a bit and then he quickly moves it into forward. The tire spins but its making ground and the car finally thrusts forward. They head back down the street and Ladro says, "Thank God. We probably would've died up here once the wolves came out to eat."

"Wolves? Where the hell do ya think you are, Canada?"

"We gotta be close."

About a half a mile later, they notice a huge sign secured by two concrete pillars that says, The Baseball Compound. The sign is about six feet tall by fifteen feet wide and the lettering is in navy blue. A three foot brick wall runs on both sides with mums planted in front making the entrance appear grand.

Ladro turns into the complex and they head down a long parking lot packed with cars. "Holy shit. Look at this place." Nutsy's amazed at the size of it. It's like an amusement park for baseball players.

Even Ladro is amazed at the size and activity and replies, "Wow, this is even bigger than my vision in the hospital was."

Nutsy is in complete awe. He can't believe the amount of cars and people wandering around. The complex is spotless, much different than the complex he's been used to staring at.

As they slowly move through the parking lot searching for a parking space, Nutsy glances toward the baseball fields off to the side. Baseball players are scattered across the fields while crowds loudly cheer them on.

Ladro finally finds a parking space and they both step out of the car and head toward the main entrance. When they arrive, a lady in a booth says, "Ten dollars each, please."

Ladro asks, "To just walk in?"

"Yes, sir."

So Nutsy hands the lady a twenty dollar bill and asks, "We're looking for someone. How can we find the team?"

The lady points toward a large, one level modern building in the middle of the park and replies, "Go to the main building and the schedules are posted on one of the TV monitors."

"Thanks," Nutsy replies.

They both head toward the large structure passing parents and their kids dressed in uniforms with all different team names. Most players are carrying large bat bags. Nutsy's taking it all in. Maybe this has been the missing piece to his puzzle, the piece that could make his dream profitable.

They finally enter the main building with tan vinyl siding and notice a food court area with tables and chairs to relax on or eat at.

On one end of the large room are ten batting cages for teams to take swings in before their games. Nutsy and Ladro pause in front of a TV monitor on a wall. "What's the name of the team?" Ladro asks.

So Nutsy pulls a piece of paper from his pants pocket and takes a look at it. "Duchess Lightning."

"That's a pretty cool name."

Nutsy laughs and replies, "Oh, there's something ya finally like?"

"Nutsy, do you know how much action we can take in at a place like this?" Ladro's wheels are spinning.

"What's wrong with you? No one bets these games."

"Maybe, we can be the first to offer it."

"Let's go. They're on field five. Besides, these are kids."

Nutsy and Ladro leave the main building and head down a concrete path toward a field that's in the back section of the complex.

"It's over there," Nutsy nods toward the other side.

So Nutsy and Ladro change direction and head down another concrete path toward another field. They finally make it to field five and stand behind bleachers with mostly parents watching. "I don't see him," Nutsy says.

Presto just finished going to the bathroom and notices Nutsy and Ladro standing by the field. "I see they'll let anyone in this complex," Presto sarcastically says.

Nutsy and Ladro both turn and Nutsy says, "Yeah, imagine that?" Nutsy exchanges a handshake with Presto. "Ya remember Larry?"

Ladro and Presto exchange a handshake and Presto says, "How can I not? We spent a few rough weekends down at the shore together."

"I think I'm still paying for some of those weekends."

"Aren't we all?" Nutsy replies.

"Hey, I'm glad you guys came."

"I gotta say, you're right. I'm impressed," Nutsy replies.

Presto peeks at his watch and says, "I got about five minutes and then we start the next game."

"Did you win?" Ladro asks.

"Nah, a kid on the other team hit a walk off homer. So, Nutsy, this is what I was telling you about. There's four big fields and three fifty by seventy fields."

"What's fifty by seventy?"

"When the players turn eleven, they play on a larger field than little league so they can lead and steal."

"Do the pitchers still wind up?"

"No, they have to learn how to pitch from the stretch."

"Wow, that's much different from when we played," Ladro replies.

"It's not even in the same ballpark," Presto replies.

"What about the teams? Where do they come from?"

"All over, most from out of state. If it's a big tournament, they have to stay over a few nights."

"Who pays for that?" Nutsy asks.

"That's on the parents."

"Shit, and people really do this?" Nutsy asks.

"Every week… look at all the fields and players." Nutsy and Ladro glance around the complex in amazement.

Tammy, Presto's wife, heads toward them and says, "I think they need you on the field." She glances at Nutsy and says, "Sorry to interrupt."

"No problem, nice to see ya again."

Tammy smiles and walks away. She is not one bit happy to see Nutsy and Ladro up here. She always believed her husband missed the action from his old city and that Nutsy and Ladro would just drag him back in somehow.

"I gotta get back on the field. Why don't you stick around and come back to the house for a drink. I'm about fifteen minutes from here."

"Next time. We gotta head back soon… I'd like to stay in touch. I got some questions for ya."

Presto's cell phone rings and he peeks at the display showing Salvatore's name. "Shit, this guy. Excuse me one second." Presto answers, "Yeah, Squalo."

Nutsy and Ladro catch eyes.

Presto says, "Squalo, I told you the premium –"

Squalo interrupts Presto and Presto's eyes roll. "That's up to you," Presto replies and hangs up with an annoyed look on his face.

"What's Squalo calling you for?" Nutsy asks.

"I insured the building Belinda was running… you heard Leo's out, right?"

Ladro replies, "Yeah, we know."

"He's blaming me for the place not being insured when it burnt down."

"When?" Nutsy asks.

"Apparently, the other day… down to the ground… call me, the game's starting." Presto exchanges a handshake with Nutsy and Ladro and then heads toward the dugout.

Since Presto's in the insurance business, a vision of the young girl from the cemetery flashes through Nutsy's mind and he says, "Presto, let me ask ya a quick question."

"Yeah," Presto turns back.

"This lady from the neighborhood's husband applied for life insurance but got into a car accident before the process was finished."

"Oh shit, that's terrible. Was the accident before or after the process ended?"

"I'm not sure. Why? Does it make a difference?"

"Did she put down a binder?"

"I think so. She mentioned the company sent a check back."

"It might... give her my number. I'll see if I can help her out. I gotta go." Presto heads into the dugout.

Nutsy and Ladro wander toward a concession stand and Ladro asks, "Are you talking about the plumber's wife?"

"Yeah, I can't get her daughter out of my mind. Let's get a hot dog and watch some of the game," Nutsy says.

"Shit, Squalo must be fuming about the shop," Ladro says.

"Fuck him. I hope his apartment burns down next."

They walk up to a concession stand and Ladro scans the price list. "Jesus Christ, four dollars for a fucking hot dog?"

"Stop complaining, will ya? I got it."

A lady behind the counter asks, "Can I help you?"

"Nutsy replies, "Yeah, we'll take two hot dogs and two coffees.""

Ladro cuts in, "You know what, make it four hot dogs."

So Nutsy eyes Ladro and sarcastically replies, "Yeah sure, what the hell. I'm paying, right?"

Ladro laughs and asks the lady, "Is the coffee fresh?"

"Yes, it's a new pot."

"Alright good. Throw some muffins in there too."

"Anything else?" Nutsy asks with an annoyed look.

"What kind, sir?"

"Throw in a few blueberry and corn."

The lady presses buttons on a cash register and says, "That's twenty-four dollars."

Ladro turns away and laughs.

Leo finally talked Squalo into fronting him the money for some pistols. Well, not really. Leo had told him it was for an apartment he had secured. He knows Squalo wants him out so he figured this would be a good time to hit him up for some cash. Leo sits on Squalo's terrace and calls Miguel who answers at his office, "What's up, Leo?"

"Tell that dickhead friend of yours, I'll take twenty."

"Twenty what?"

"I'll text you the info over four different texts. I need them by tonight. I gotta start making money again."

"That's a lot of money. How are you paying?"

"Just tell him at our old place." Leo hangs up without answering.

Squalo roams onto the terrace and asks, "When are you signing the lease?"

"Next week."

Squalo nods and heads back into the apartment. He can't wait for Leo to get out. He calls Donnola but the phone just keeps ringing again. "What did this asshole jump off a bridge after the game?"

Papo strolls through one of his towers with an architect, an engineer, and a city building inspector. The city inspector has been busting his balls about the metal mesh going under the concrete floors. They are arguing over the thickness. Papo thinks he's fine with it, but the inspector wants it thicker.

The engineer and architect agree with Papo, but the inspector keeps on insisting for a thicker wire. Paulie yells out from a distance, "The concrete truck should be here in about an hour or so!" One of Paulie's associates supplies Papo with the concrete.

"Call him up and tell him to forget today. We got an issue!" Papo replies.

"What issue?" Paulie asks while approaching them.

"We might have to switch out the wire mesh for the concrete."

"Why?"

Papo nods toward the building inspector and says, "Because he said so."

"Who's he?" Paulie has never seen this inspector before.

"The new city inspector."

"It's what we always used," Paulie replies with a nasty tone.

"The code changed," the inspector sternly replies.

"You can't change it mid-term. That's bullshit." Paulie asks the engineer, "This was all approved, right?"

"Right down to the last bolt," the engineer replies.

"It doesn't matter. It needs to be changed." The inspector moves away.

So Paulie loses his patience and yells out, "Hey, hold up a minute."

Papo says, "Paulie, forget it."

Paulie ignores Papo's comment and gets in the inspector's face. "When did you start?"

"A few weeks ago."

"Well, you better sharpen your pencil because this fucking concrete is getting poured today. It's paid for already."

"No it ain't."

Paulie whips out his phone and calls Billy who's currently sitting with Gloria in her outdoor hot tub set on a slate patio. Billy grabs his phone and answers, "What's up, Paulie?"

"Do you know this new piece of shit inspector?"

"Not really, why?"

"We got over ten concrete trucks on the way and he's telling us the wire mesh needs to be changed."

"Wasn't this all approved beforehand?"

"Yeah, that's what I said but he's insisting. Can you talk to this moron?"

"Why, he's there?"

"Yeah."

So Paulie hands his phone off to the inspector and the inspector says, "I don't know who this is but –"

Billy cuts him off. "This is William Manza. Who's this?"

"William Manza? The guy who headed the party a few years back?"

"That's right. What seems to be the issue here today?"

"They don't have the proper mesh."

"I'll tell you what. You take another look at your file that's already been cleared by the city for months now. If you still insist it needs to be changed, then I'll have a talk with the mayor, and if you just happen to be wrong, I'll have your job and make sure you never work in this city again… if you're right, we'll change it… deal?"

"Hold on… all I know is the wire needs to be thicker."

"I asked you a simple question. You're the inspector, not me."

While the inspector thinks it over, Billy asks, "Who put you up to this?"

"No one, why?"

"Because no inspector in their right mind walks on an approved job busting balls like this. So, you're either working for someone or looking for something. Which is it?"

The inspector hesitantly replies, "I'll let the trucks come."

The inspector hands the phone back to Paulie and bolts away. "Can you imagine this shit, Billy?"

"Where is this guy from?"

"He looks like a slime ball city guy."

"Alright, we gotta find out who's behind him. I'll call you later." Billy hangs up.

"Who was that?" Gloria asks.

"It looks like we might have another inspector planted in this city."

"Great… that's all we need right now."

"We'll take care of him like the last one."

Gloria wiggles over toward Billy and rests her arms on top of his shoulders while facing him. "You sounded sexy on the phone the way you put your words."

"You think so?"

"I know so." Gloria leans in for a kiss.

CHAPTER 19

Binky and Belo have decided to meet up on their own for various reasons at Belo's shop on Central Park Avenue. One in particular, for the meeting they had with Nutsy. They are currently in the back of Belo's shop in a small dated kitchenette and Binky says, "Look, we all know Nutsy wants out if his idea works. AND it's in our best interest to help him achieve it."

"I still can't believe he would do this… it's a lot to walk away from after all these years."

"It is and it's not. It just depends on where your mind is at."

"Yeah, I guess… how do you feel about the thirty percent cut he wants?"

"Listen, don't start this shit again. Our seventy percent and controlling the area is better than no percent, isn't it?"

"I'm just asking. He'll be getting thirty for no risk."

"I'll tell you what. I'll ask Squalo then, how about that? I fucking brought you and Nutsy back together and you're starting this shit?"

"Binky, take it easy. I'm only asking."

"Well, don't ask again."

Leo, Miguel, and Big Charlie are currently in the back of a dilapidated warehouse on the westside that Miguel is attempting to develop into townhouses. Big Charlie has been an investor in Miguel's construction projects over the years and is curious about this residential project Miguel currently has in front of the planning board. This one would be like a small village within itself, with its own shops and restaurants and hundreds of townhouses and condos.

Leo's shop burning down has changed his situation with Miguel. Leo was planning on financing the shop and use the money as an investor in Miguel's project. Now with the insurance in question, Leo feels he's stuck and no bank will finance his business. He's becoming somewhat anxious and it's out of character for him.

Besides taking a glimpse at the site, Leo and Big Charlie agreed beforehand to twenty pistols at eight hundred a piece and have decided to make the swap here.

Big Charlie is holding a pillowcase full of guns and Leo has a backpack that's full of cash. Big Charlie has become aware that Leo is attempting to invest in the project and is not currently happy with the idea. "He can't come in on this project," Big Charlie says to Miguel.

Miguel asks, "Why not?" Miguel knows very well that Leo is not a good investor to have on his list but feels he has no choice.

"He's a known criminal. You'll lose the project and your reputation with him on the list."

Leo asks with an annoyed look, "Why, you're a saint now?"

Big Charlie replies, "No, but my name is spotless, not like yours. You're a known felon."

"You know something LITTLE Charlie, you act like you're some big man or something, but you're still a little shit."

Big Charlie gets in Leo's face and replies, "You wanna see how little?"

Miguel cuts in, "Alright, make the deal and let's go. I have a meeting to attend."

Leo and Big Charlie lock eyes. They are both not giving in to each other and Miguel knows it. "Let's finish I said." Miguel just wants to get out of here.

"How much you got on you?" Big Charlie asks.

"I got sixteen for them all," Leo replies even though he has nowhere near that amount. He's just sizing Big Charlie up.

"How many you got in the sack?" Leo asks.

Miguel gets an uncomfortable feeling since he can notice a twinge in Leo's eyes, a twinge he's seen before and it wasn't pretty what had happened afterwards. "We can finish another day. I gotta go," Miguel insists.

"I'm buying these right now," Leo replies with a stern voice.

So Leo and Big Charlie lock eyes again while both having an uncomfortable feeling. Big Charlie's hand begins to slip inside his jacket while a strap falls down from Leo's sleeve. Leo is incredibly quick and agile, so he spins around and is able to wrap the strap around Big Charlie's neck. Miguel can't believe what's happening and says, "Let him go."

Leo squeezes tightly as Big Charlie anxiously attempts to remove the strap, but Leo has a firm grip and Big Charlie cannot break free. All the years of working out in the courtyard has given Leo amazing strength.

Miguel becomes nervous and glances around to see if anyone is near. They are all alone in a desolate area of this abandoned site. Leo's eyes fire up as he squeezes tighter.

Squalo stands with a building superintendent in front of Donnola's front door. "I've been calling him for days. It's not like him."

"Maybe he took a trip," the super replies.

"Nah, this guy's too cheap to go anywhere."

The super pulls a large key ring from his jacket pocket and sorts through it. He finally finds Donnola's spare key and opens the door. At first, they are both taken aback by the stench of the apartment. "Jesus Christ. It smells horrible in here," Squalo says while holding his nose.

They both enter the dark apartment since all the blinds are drawn and pause in shock. Donnola is sprawled out on the living room floor with dried up blood around his head on the dirty carpet. "Holy fuck!" Squalo yells out.

The super nervously whips out his phone and dials 911.

Leo is now dragging Big Charlie's body toward a section with overgrown grass, weeds, and bushes by the warehouse. He pulls Big Charlie into a thick section of brush and rotted piles of wood.

Leo heads back to where Miguel is nervously waiting and says, "You make sure everyone knows I'm back and I mean business. You got that?" Besides hitting Big Charlie up for the pistols, Leo wanted Miguel to witness his violent behavior and prove to him he's not playing around. "You got me?" Leo asks again with a stern voice.

Miguel just nods yes and remains quiet. Big Charlie has been a solid investor and still had a stellar reputation on paper that helped Miguel tremendously with his projects. He now feels Leo will be nothing but a thorn in his side, and Miguel knows he's desperate for cash.

Leo picks up the pillowcase and says, "Let's get outta here."

"You're just gonna leave him like that?"

"Yeah, fuck 'im."

Blackie and Belinda are having a quick drink at a local diner across the street from the bank. Belinda couldn't be happier that she started her new career and path in life. They are sipping from wine glasses and talking about old times.

A city detective enters the diner and eyes Blackie from a distance and moves toward her table. He questioned both Squalo and Leo earlier knowing they are both part of the shop and Squalo had told him Vito had a major issue with Blackie a few weeks ago. Squalo also knew about the incident Vito had with Sammy at the bar and made sure the detective was well aware of it.

So the detective stands by their table and says, "I need a few minutes of your time." He knows Blackie very well.

"For what?" Blackie asks.

"We understand both you and your niece had an issue with the young man we just found in the woods."

"What young man?" Blackie asks.

"Vito Rena, from her shop." The detective nods toward Belinda.

So Blackie's eyes open wide and she asks, "What do you mean they found him in the woods?"

"His body was badly beaten and dumped in the bushes."

"Well, that has nothing to do with me. You should be questioning her brother." Blackie nods toward Belinda.

"I already discussed this with him. Where were you . . .?"

Blackie interrupts him. "I was at the hospital with my husband who got smashed over the head by a burglar in my house, that's where. How about asking me how you could help catch that person?" Right now, she can't believe Belinda had known this and didn't tell her.

"We're working on that also… what time did you leave?"

"When I left, that's when." Blackie is livid that the detective seems more concerned about questioning her about Vito than her husband's situation.

"I can see you don't want to cooperate."

"I'll cooperate when you find the person who broke into my house and almost killed MY husband, that's when."

"Thank you for your time. We'll be talking again," the detective sarcastically says while moving toward the exit.

Blackie glances toward Belinda with a pissed off look. "I was waiting for the right time to tell you, Blackie, I swear."

"This kind of news never has a right time."

"Blackie, I swear –"

Blackie tosses money on the table and says, "Let's go." Blackie stands up and storms out. Belinda was going to tell her, but she wanted to make sure her position was secured at the bank first. She was planning on discussing this with Blackie right after the work day was over, but the detective beat her to it.

Presto sits in the dugout with the other coach and the players. His cell phone rings and he answers, "Presto!"

On the other end is an investigator from the insurance carrier the body shop was insured with. "Hi, this is Susan from the Texco Insurance Company. I need a few minutes of your time."

"Sure, please make it quick. I'm in the middle of my son's baseball game."

"Well, sir, I have to complete an investigation."

"For what?" Presto asks while stepping out of the dugout and off the field.

"A customer said he gave you eight-thousand dollars in cash for his insurance policy and you never handed in the premium."

"What customer?"

"Salvatore DeSanto."

Presto's eyes roll. He knows exactly where this is heading. "He never gave me cash and told me he didn't want the insurance anymore."

"Do you have that in writing?"

"I'm not sure." Presto knows damn well he doesn't since Squalo got annoyed and hung up on him that day.

"Well, we have a business that's burnt to the ground and their six-hundred thousand dollar coverage is currently void."

"How is that my issue?"

"If he gave you the money and you –"

"I told you already, he gave me nothing!" Presto is annoyed.

"Okay, we'll have to complete a full investigation on this matter."

"Do whatever you have to do." Presto hangs up and heads
back into the dugout.

CHAPTER 20

Nutsy and Ladro are heading back home on the parkway. They are both impressed by not only the baseball complex, but the amount of activity. Nutsy thinks this could possibly be his missing link to the sports complex. The park he's eyeing is close to a parkway with a large empty lot next door that could be turned into a multi-level parking garage. "What are you thinking?" Ladro asks while noticing Nutsy gazing out of the window.

"This could be it, Ladro, the final piece to the puzzle. Imagine the profit they make at that place?"

"This would cost a fortune to build. The turf alone would kill us."

"Yeah, we'd have to pull everyone we know into this."

"It would take a lot to run this and the shop together."

"We'd give the shop up. I promised Billy if this ever worked out, I'd walk away."

"I'll run it. I don't giva shit."

"Nah, you'd be out too."

"Maybe I don't wanna get out. Have you ever thought about that?"

Nutsy didn't want to discuss this scenario with Ladro at this time, so he changes the topic, "Look at these trees, just beautiful... I gotta say, this place is growing on me up here."

"Don't change the topic. Suppose I don't wanna leave?"

Nutsy hesitantly replies, "We'd sell to Binky if it works out."

"Binky? Where the fuck did this come from?"

"Things need to change, Ladro. We've been lucky so far. We're pressing the envelope now."

"Lucky? How do you figure that? We sweat every fucking week out like two pigs."

"I don't think pigs sweat. Besides... weren't ya the one who told me in the hospital, ya wanna be a legend?"

"Sure, throw this in my face now."

"Well, this might finally be our chance to... I can see it now on the concession stand board, Larry's Hot Dog."

"Fuck that... my name ain't going on a hot dog. If anything, it's going on the cheese steak sandwich. AND, I don't like the idea of you making deals without me knowing. This is bullshit, Nutsy."

"We've been friends forever and you're my brother-in-law. If I'm out, you're out. It's that simple... pull over, I gotta take a piss. That coffee went right through me."

"If I'm out you're out? What kind of horseshit is that? I ain't your boyfriend."

"Just pull over, will ya?"

Billy has decided to visit Papo at his apartment on the north side. He wants to make sure Papo understands exactly what's been currently on his mind lately. Papo will probably not be happy to hear it, but Billy doesn't care.

After Billy rings the buzzer, Papo answers the door and is somewhat taken aback to see Billy. "Is everything all right?"

"Yeah, fine. You got a minute?"

"Come in." Papo opens the door to allow Billy in and closes the door behind him.

Billy follows Papo into his kitchen and they both take a seat at the table. "What's on your mind, Billy? And thanks for straightening out that inspector."

"No problem... alright, listen. I've known you forever and respect you as a man, but I'm gonna say something you're probably not gonna like."

"Hey, we're all adults here, right? I stopped taking things personally a long time ago."

"This ain't personal."

"Shoot, Billy."

"I want you to lay off Nuccio."

"I'm not following you."

"I don't want him involved with anything further like the past... you follow that?"

"Listen, Billy, everyone thinks –"

Billy cuts him off, "It's not my concern what everyone thinks and I'm not asking you what happened, but I'm telling you Nutsy doesn't get involved with anything new."

Papo becomes somewhat defensive and asks, "Are you making Nutsy's decisions now?"

"If that's what you wanna call it, go ahead. But whatever's going through YOUR mind, count him out."

"Remember one thing, Billy, you can change the appearance of a person but you can't change who they are down deep inside."

"Get your brother this time if need be. He'll be glad to get involved."

"Yeah sure, and give up two square miles to his family… I don't think so."

"Then that's how it has to go… Nuccio stays out this time."

Papo turns away and remains quiet.

The detective investigating Vito's case bangs on Nutsy's front door. Sammy and Bono are watching TV together in the living room. Sammy still has the ice wrap on her ankle. The swelling is reducing but taking a long time, longer than she has patience for. "N-J, grab the door," Sammy yells out.

So N-J opens the front door. The detective stands on the step and says, "I'm looking to speak to Samantha Gento, is she here?"

Since N-J is always protective of Sammy, he asks with a serious tone, "Who are you?"

"I'm Detective Dons and I need to ask her a few questions."

Kathy appears behind N-J after overhearing the detective's comment and asks, "About what?"

"We're investigating a situation and need to rule her out."

"What investigation?"

"We found a young man dead in the woods."

N-J flips out and yells, "It wasn't my sister! You get the hell out of here before –"

Kathy cuts him off, "N-J, that's enough. Go inside."

N-J stares the Detective down and Kathy continues on, "I said go inside. Now!"

N-J turns and storms away back into the kitchen. "He better not touch my sister," N-J mumbles under his breath.

Kathy says, "I would rather you speak with her when my husband is present."

"Is he close by?"

Kathy pulls her phone out from her pants pocket and calls Nutsy.

⚬⚬

Nutsy heads back toward Ladro's car after making a pit stop at a rest area. He's holding two more cups of coffee. Ladro is back and forth with the news Nutsy had told him. He likes the idea of getting out, but he also doesn't like the idea of giving the operation away.

What Ladro doesn't know yet and eventually Nutsy will tell him, is the hit Binky and Belo had performed on Donnola. They all knew Donnola had to go and Nutsy's still attempting to keep his hands clean. It's not a secret that Nutsy and Donnola did not like each other, so Nutsy thought it would be the best avenue at this point in time.

Nutsy gets back into the car and hands off a coffee container to Ladro. "So, why Binky?" Ladro asks since it's still on his mind.

"Who else would we give it to?"

"That's a good question."

"That's what I'm saying. We don't have too many choices and Binky's always been a stand-up guy."

"Don't kid yourself, it's only because we don't compete with him."

"Nah, Binky's alright... I gotta say, it would be a nice change hangin' out at ballfields again. Kinda like years back."

Ladro hits the gas and they continue back on the parkway heading south. Nutsy's cell phone rings and he answers, "What's up?"

"Where are you?" Kathy asks while standing by the front door with the detective.

"I'm on the parkway heading back."

"I called you three times already."

"I didn't hear anything, probably bad service where I am."

"Well, you better get home. A detective wants to ask Sammy a few questions."

"About what?"

"That kid Vito was found in the woods on the north side of town."

"What?! Why her then?"

"I don't know. I'm standing outside of the house with him right now."

"Put him on."

"My husband would like to talk to you."

The detective takes the phone from Kathy and says, "It's just a formality. We have to cross the names off the list."

"Why is her name on the list?"

"Because of their incident at the bar last week."

"What incident?"

"Apparently, she roughed him up the other night."

Nutsy doesn't want to appear startled and replies, "So what? Ya never had a fight before? It's not a crime, ya know."

"I just need to cross names off my list. That's it."

"Then cross it off."

"You know I have to ask the questions."

"Come back in an hour when I'm home."

The detective peeks at his watch and asks, "Alright, how about five?"

"I'll have donuts waiting."

"Yeah thanks," the detective sarcastically replies and hands off the phone to Kathy. "I'll be back later. Please tell your daughter not to go anywhere."

Kathy nervously watches the detective head back towards his car that is double parked on the street.

Nutsy finishes the call with an annoyed look and Ladro asks, "What happened?"

"It looks like your friend already got what was coming to him?"

"Leo?"

"No, the punk."

"Are you shitting me?! Then again, it's not surprising with his cocky attitude."

"They wanna question Sammy about it." Nutsy wipes his forehead.

"Why her?"

"Who the hell knows… hit the gas, I wanna be there when this prick comes back."

Ladro presses down hard on the pedal and replies, "It never ends, Nutsy."

"No it doesn't, does it?" Nutsy gazes out of the passenger window. "Look at us. Ya got a bandage on your head, my shoulders are all screwed up… and ya wonder why everyone's gettin' the fuck outta the city and movin' north."

"Yeah, looks that way."

"I'm thinkin' of keepin' N-J home for a while."

"Who's gonna watch him?"

"Kathy wants to leave her job so she'd be able to."

"Shit, she's got the benefits. Besides, I thought he was happy there."

"Nah, he's faking it."

"How do you know?"

"He told me… he's way too young to be miserable."

"I agree… imagine when he's our age then?"

Squalo makes a phone call while standing outside of Donnola's apartment. He can't believe what he had just witnessed inside. Belo answers his phone while still conversing with Binky in his office. "What's up, Squalo?"

"The weasel took a few bullets to the head."

Belo laughs while attempting to play it off and Squalo sternly says, "I'm not fucking kidding."

"What are you talking about?" Belo still attempts to be surprised.

"I'm talking about keeping your eyes open behind your back. It could be you or me next." Squalo hangs up and heads toward his parked car.

Leo stands in front of his charred shop with an intense glare. The shop is now one large pile of rubble. Detective Dons pulls up and gets out of his car. Leo turns and asks, "You pin anyone yet?"

"Not yet. I'm working on it."

"Well, work harder."

"You got my cash?"

"I plan on collecting soon, even if I gotta get it from Blackie."

"They still think you shot Ladro's brother?"

"Yeah, don't worry. You're still clear... am I clear with this kid yet?"

Detective Dons opens his car door and replies, "You're crossed off the list." Detective Dons slides into his car. "I'll be expecting my money soon. I waited long enough." The car takes off.

Leo puckers his lips and glares back at the shop.

Nutsy wipes his forehead while waiting in the passenger seat for Ladro to finish going to the bathroom on the side of the parkway. After finishing, Ladro tramples through high grass heading back toward his car and Nutsy sarcastically says, "Maybe ya do need a rubber band. That's like your tenth piss already."

"Nah, my bladder's fine. It's the shitty coffee up here." Ladro gets in and they take off heading south.

"Ya know if we chase this, we got one shot at it."

"Yeah, I know. What detective came to the house?"

"It sounded like that asshole that used to hit on Blackie years back."

"Are you talking about Leo's old buddy?"

Nutsy just nods yes and wipes his forehead again.

"I thought he retired. What rock did he crawl out from?"

Nutsy gazes out of the window and replies, "I don't know. All I know is life is gettin' tiring, Ladro."

"I know what you mean."

"Do me a favor, put the heat down. I'm dyin' in here." Nutsy wipes his forehead again.

"It's not on… why are you sweating so much?"

Nutsy cracks the window and replies, "With my luck, my cut's probably infected."

"Maybe it's a good thing you did give Munchie the money back. I think you better go see him at his office. Your color's off."

"For whatever reason I can't see this through, promise me ya will to the end."

"Nutsy, don't start this bullshit –"

"Just fuckin' promise me!"

"Of course I will."

"Good. Now that ya know my plan, I hope ya don't put the malocchio on me."

Ladro laughs and replies, "If I was gonna screw you, I would've done it already."

"Is that so?"

"Yeah, that's so. You should only know how loyal I've been to you."

"I do, Ladro, more than ya know."

"Holy shit! Now I know you ain't feeling good for sure. You agreed with me for once."

While Nutsy just laughs it off, Ladro continues, "You never gave me an answer from before."

"About what? Ya asked me a thousand and one questions."

"Your dream, is it the same vision I had in the hospital?"

Nutsy nods yes and replies, "Very close. Now, I just gotta make sure the detective doesn't pin anything on Sammy."

Made in the USA
Coppell, TX
08 March 2021